A SEA WASHED VICTORY

Forgotten Gods: Book Three

LEAH R CUTTER

Knotted Road Press

A Sea Washed Victory
Forgotten Gods: Book Three
Copyright © 2020 Leah Cutter
All rights reserved
Published by Knotted Road Press
www.KnottedRoadPress.com

ISBN: 978-1-64470-146-1

Cover Art:

ID 3668985 © John Bigl | Dreamstime.com

Cover and interior design copyright © 2020 Knotted Road Press

http://www.KnottedRoadPress.com

Come someplace new…
Are you a traveler? Do you enjoy exploring strange new worlds, new cultures, new people?

Journey into the various lands envisioned by Leah Cutter.

Sign up for my newsletter and I'll start you on your travels with a free copy of my book, *The Island Sampler*.

I will never spam you or use your email for nefarious purposes. You can also unsubscribe at any time.

http://www.LeahCutter.com/newsletter/

Forgotten Gods

A Wind Blown Torment

A Stone Strewn Clash

A Sea Washed Victory

Tanish Empire Trilogy

The Glass Magician

The Desert Heart

The Ghost Dog

The Cassie Stories

Poisoned Pearls

Tainted Waters

Spoiled Harvest

Bloodied Ice

The Witch's Progress

Circle of Air

Circle of Water

Circle of Fire

Circle of Earth

Seattle Trolls

The Changeling Troll

The Princess Troll

The Fairy-Bridge Troll

The Troll-Demon War

The Troll-Human War

The Troll-Troll War

The Shadow Wars Trilogy

The Raven and the Dancing Tiger

The Guardian Hound

War Among the Crocodiles

The Clockwork Fairy Kingdom

The Clockwork Fairy Kingdom

The Maker, the Teacher, and the Monster

The Dwarven Wars

The Chronicles of Franklin

Franklin Versus The Popcorn Thief

Franklin Versus The Soul Thief

Franklin Versus The Child Thief

Huli Intergalactic - Science/Space Fantasy

Origins

The Strawberry Girl

Contemporary Fantasy

Siren's Call

The Immortals' War

Chapter One

____

WIND

SMOKE STILL WREATHED the air three weeks after the burning of Shan Yu, the capital of the Wind People. Gan Ou growled low in her throat every time she got a good snoutful, remembering the battle there.

The Wind People had been outnumbered by the Bone People.

Still were.

Gan Ou wished she could enjoy the slow coming of spring, finally back in her homeland. The nights were still cold, frost sparkling on the edges of dried grass and ice forming across the tops of shallow puddles. While it might snow some nights, the days brought warmth and rain. Buds were starting to pop up on the bushes and trees, already bringing green to the land and warming Gan Ou's heart. A few overly eager crocuses had already poked out of the earth, though it was too early for them yet.

But Gan Ou was too involved with the war to spend time gardening. The Wind People had been fighting the Bone People for well over a month, trying to stop them from sweeping from their lands to those of the Stone People. They were now four days west of the burned-out capital and losing ground every day.

For the battle that day, Gan Ou transformed into her favorite shape, that of a great gray wolf. She stood over four feet tall at the shoulders, the claws on her four paws wickedly sharp. She'd extended her canines a bit as well, giving her a deadly bite. The world grayed out as she changed, her eyes losing dominance as her sense of smell expanded, bringing in details she'd missed earlier, like how the wind smelled of rain underneath the smoke, and that there were still deer in the woods nearby.

She growled at the warriors closest to her, those who had chosen to follow this stubborn old coot into battle. They growled back, ready to bite, tear, and rend the Bone People.

They'd learned to work in pairs—a large attack animal such as a wolf or a bear with a much smaller creature at its side, who could drag away any of the nets that the Bone People threw. Gan Ou worked with Io Mon, a dour young man as pessimistic as she was. They were a good match, him preferring a small, mud-colored terrier with extra strong jaws.

Hundreds of Wind People filled the clearing, the sounds of many animals now ringing through the air. The field of battle had been chosen and the Wind People had brought in many recruits this time. They had divided themselves up into groups, some planning on nipping at the flanks of their enemy instead of all of them rushing head on, as they had last time.

Would it be enough to stop the Bone People? To halt their steady progression across the Wind People's territory? The Bone People gained territory after almost every battle.

Probably not. They'd probably lose again, and forfeit yet another field.

Gan Ou doubted that anything the Wind People did that day would be enough. The Bone People seemed unstoppable.

However, she considered her pessimism an advantage. Unlike the youngsters, Gan Ou wasn't heartbroken and disappointed that the Wind People hadn't stopped the Bone People before now.

During the first large skirmish, she'd refused to leave the battlefield until the last of those she'd fought beside had given way. Not because she believed they'd win, but because her age made her more stubborn than most. She just wouldn't give up and turn aside when the others did.

Despite how the elders wouldn't listen to Gan Ou, she'd gathered a cohort of warriors to her. Not the bravest of the lot, just those who had the potential of being as unwavering as a determined old woman.

If any of them lived long enough.

Gan Ou led her group to the southwest corner of the meadow chosen for that day's battle. This morning was one of those times when she was happy for her banishment. The field in front of her held no special meaning, unlike some of the others who remembered picnics or dancing in ceremonies there. It was just another fighting ground, someplace else where she and the others could slaughter their enemy.

And be slaughtered in return.

Sunlight made the tips of the wet grass sparkle—at least in the patches that were still standing, that hadn't been trampled or turned into mud from a previous battle. A long line of Bone People formed up on the other side of the field. Many of them also gleamed in the sunlight, their bone armor protecting them.

It was a much larger group of opponents than the Wind People had been expecting.

Seemed that the Bone People had also brought in reinforcements.

Fear made Gan Ou's hackles rise up along her spine. Her

stomach twisted, cold and heavy. She found herself growling without intending to.

The wind carried the ash scent of the Bone People to her. She didn't bother counting how many individuals there were, just how many priests.

The elders of the Wind People had passed along an order that the warriors needed to focus on killing as many priests that day as possible. While the Wind People didn't really have any war elders—each group fought on their own—it seemed as though for the Bone People, the priests directed them, their messages carried on dark clouds.

Gan Ou had been surprised how quickly she'd been able to pick up the wind speech that was native to her people. Some could only hear words carried on the wind, while Gan Ou found that she could easily form them. It gave her yet another advantage during the battles.

It was much more difficult to speak with the wind when Gan Ou was transformed. She was one of the few who could, though. She tagged the scent of the priest that she intended to target, and sent it to the rest of her group.

The growls and nods she got in return settled her nerves. Io Mon, in his terrier form, came up to stand beside her.

She wasn't alone in her quest. That, in turn, made her even more stubborn.

She would kill one of those damned priests today.

Or die trying.

THE GREAT CLASH between the two armies as they raced across the field felt almost normal now to Gan Ou. The sounds of howls of creatures intermingled with the grunts and shouts of men. How the smell of blood poured into the air almost immediately. The taste of her own fear as she ran, knocking over the first individual she met, then leaping aside before a knife found her back.

During previous battles, the priests of the Bone People had called up fog and smoke, making it difficult to attack. This morning, they hadn't bothered hiding themselves. All they'd conjured was hard armor for their warriors and cold, six-foot spears for themselves.

Their arrogance would be their undoing, at least as far as Gan Ou was concerned.

The scent of the priest was closer than she expected. He must have come running forward with the rest of his warriors instead of hanging back. Gan Ou could almost taste his flesh, painted in ashes. It took her a moment to send a word to her cohort, to get them to follow her. She ducked under a net thrown her direction. Another opponent appeared at her side, a heavy blow to her back making her yelp.

She turned away from her target, toward her attacker. He had a net ready in his hands. Gan Ou still leaped at him, throwing the weight of her body across the space.

While she knew that the winds didn't actually pick her up and carry her the last few feet, it sometimes felt as if they did.

Her momentum along with her weight carried Gan Ou and her opponent to the ground. She heard his ribs crack and he gasped.

Not allowing herself to think, Gan Ou tore out his throat with a sharp snap of her teeth. Then she was up and on her paws before the cursed net that the dead warrior carried drained any more power from her. She paused for a moment, shaking herself, as if she'd just come in from the rain and was trying to throw the water from her fur.

She heard Han Su's call in the distance. Gan Ou raced toward him.

Crap.

The priest had his damned bone wand out in front of him. A long pike of blue was forming, aimed directly at the heart of the bear lumbering toward him.

Gan Ou couldn't see Han Su's partner anywhere. The smaller creatures sometimes had trouble keeping up during melee.

Suddenly, a hawk launched itself at the priest's eyes. Han Su's partner.

The priest jerked back, raising the spear. It cut through the air. Feathers flew.

Han Su roared and rushed forward.

Gan Ou had no time to tell him to pause.

The youngster threw himself at the priest, only to be cut in two by that damned blue spear.

However, while the priest was busy trying to defend himself from the front attacker, Gan On leaped at him from the side.

Damn it! Where had that other warrior come from? The weight of the net on her already bruised back made her stumble.

Io Mon quickly appeared at her side, leaping up and grabbing the net with his teeth, dragging it off of her. Someone else from her group, maybe Pan Shi, rushed at the priest again, keeping that deadly spear away from her. Gan Ou leaped away, out of the immediate area.

Another loud howl as another Wind Person died.

That was it. Gan Ou had had enough.

She raced at the priest with all her might. She would swear that a wind traveled with her this time, rushing at the Bone Person and making him stagger back.

Gan Ou didn't try to leap directly at the priest. She swerved to his left, as if she were just going to try to knock him over. He brought the spear in that direction, while Io Mon jumped on him from the opposite side.

Before the priest could react to the little terrier who had firmly attached itself to his thigh, Gan Ou swerved back, keeping her leap low so that she would hit the priest close to his waist.

Others had reported that the bags that hung from the warriors belts' sometimes contained a powerful repellant. Gan Ou got a mouthful of whatever the hell it was. Though she knocked the priest to the ground, she couldn't take advantage of his helplessness as she was forced to back away, hacking and coughing.

Without meaning to, Gan Ou found herself transforming back into a Wind Person. She stood alone, naked on the field.

Just in time to see Io Mon slain, the priest using his spear to slice the little dog into two.

Gan Ou howled loudly. She'd been partnered with Io Mon since the first fights, the pair of them snarking at each other after each battle, the black humor they shared easing their pain.

His death hurt her more than she could say, as if the blood now dripping down the priest's leg also stained her own soul.

No more.

The wind carried her words all around her group. They paused in their fighting.

Though the battle still raged on around them, the air filled with howls and screams, Gan Ou felt as though she suddenly stood in the center of a tornado.

Winds coursed around her, gaining strength.

She had believed that she needed someone to teach her magic, to fill those holes that she'd only recently discovered.

She'd been wrong.

She hadn't needed a teacher.

All she'd needed was the right combination of rage and

grief.

Gan Ou pushed her winds out from around her, directly at the priest. He swung his spear from side to side, trying to cut them to shreds.

How do you stop a wind?

Gan Ou tried to direct the winds with her hands. That put too many thoughts behind what she was doing. The winds began to die. The priest looked directly at her and raised his spear, as if intending to throw it at her.

Though it went against everything she knew, Gan Ou shut her eyes and reached again for the winds. She imagined them more like hands, tearing apart the stupid priest in front of her, letting her natural instincts carry her along.

The crunch of bone made her open her eyes again. The winds had firm hold of the priest's limbs now. They had lifted him off the ground and were stretching him apart.

Gan Ou felt the horror flowing from those whom she fought with. Her cohort had never imagined this sort of magic before, this level of torture and pain.

Particularly not from one of their own.

Too bad.

Gan Ou let her rage flow. This was for Io Mon and Han Su and all the others who had died during the battle this morning.

This priest had it coming.

She made a chopping motion in the air along with a sharp nod.

The winds snapped apart.

Limbs of the priest went flying. Blood spewed everywhere.

Gan Ou transformed into a wolf immediately. It gave her cover. Made her indistinguishable from the other Wind People.

Helped her tag the scent of the next priest.

Because killing a single priest wouldn't win this battle.

No, Gan Ou was determined now to kill them all.

<hr>

BY THE END of the battle that day, Gan Ou had managed to kill six priests. She'd had to change form frequently as the warriors had started focusing on stopping any large gray wolves that they spotted, then any hyenas, then mountain cats.

Gan Ou could only imagine the terror she'd finally struck in the hearts of the Bone People, how they were being slaughtered not just by the wind, but by a naked old woman, the antithesis of everything they believed in.

In the makeshift camp the Wind People formed after the fighting was finished, Gan Ou stayed with the few survivors of her cohort, the youngsters bringing her food and water, bathing her wounds, letting her rest while they did the work.

It wasn't long before a messenger showed up at her campfire.

"The elders would speak with you," she said, bowing her head differentially.

Gan Ou nearly told her to go stuff herself. Of course, *now* the elders wanted to talk with her.

Would they listen?

Grumbling, Gan Ou pushed herself up, every single muscle in her body complaining. Gods, she was too old for this. She adjusted the simple robe she wore, belting it tighter around her waist. The cold dirt under her bare feet supported her, helping her to stiffen her spine.

"Go on," Gan Ou said, gesturing for the messenger to lead the way.

It surprised her when the other members of her cohort fell in behind her. She missed Io Mon, missed the joke he would have cracked about how they might as well all march off together to face their doom.

The messenger led them along a winding path, passing by dozens of other campfires. Gan Ou felt her muscles starting to loosen up as she walked. She wasn't ready to fight again, not yet. Not until after a good night's sleep. Still, the cool air helped wake her.

She ignored the whispers that lifted into the air at each fire as she passed. Let them talk. At least *she* had done something about those damned priests today. Even if it felt like too little, too late.

While most of the Wind People on the field had merely fires and would sleep on the ground tonight, generally in some sort of animal form, the elders had a fine tent set up for themselves, protecting them from the night and the cold. Even in the dark, it shone with a white light. Gan Ou understood that it was a symbol as much as anything else, showing the status of the elders.

Still made her grumble.

Two guards stood just outside the tent. While they allowed her to pass, they stopped the rest of her cohort.

Gan Ou paused, looking over her shoulder at them.

"I will be back soon," she promised.

Because the techniques she'd learned to kill the Bone People would be just as effective against the elders, when it came down to it.

THE TENT WAS WARM. Gan Ou felt her shoulders relaxing automatically in the welcome heat. The space itself was probably twenty-five feet square, more than big enough for her entire group to rest together out of the cold of the night.

Not that they would ever be invited in.

Oil lamps hung from the ceiling, carried there by some poor Wind Person who had been kept away from the battle. The white fabric of the tent also gave off its own glow, some fancy magic that Gan Ou wouldn't have minded learning someday.

The air smelled of fur and too many bodies gone too long without bathing. Gan Ou suspected she probably didn't smell like a rose herself. Wooden benches were arrayed in a half-circle in the center of the tent, facing the front entrance, as though the elders were still holding audience, settling farmer disputes. Cots lined the edges of the space, heaped high with comfortable bedding that just made Gan Ou grind her teeth harder. A small fire burned in the very center of the tent, the smoke magically directed straight up, out a small hole in the ceiling.

It appeared that all the elders had survived the latest battle.

Good for them.

Gan Ou planted herself in front of the group, glaring at them, daring them to do their worst.

She'd seen more awful things, done more terrible things, than any of these children.

"Welcome, Gan Ou," Hi Lop said, greeting her. The elder still had an air of serenity about her, her short brown hair shot through with gray, wearing a simple brown shirt and long black skirt that made her look even more common, unlike the rest of the posers on the council. "We have heard about your many feats this day. We would have you tell us them, rather than hear anymore second hand."

Gan Ou sniffed at them in distain. At least they'd asked.

Before she could start, a quiet wind blew between the elders. Wind speak, she knew, directed at each other, leaving her out.

One of the elders, a taller man whose hair was as gray as

her own, rose. He carried a small bench from the side and placed it on her side of the fire. "Please, sit," he instructed before he scurried back to his side.

Huh. At least they had some clue about what Gan Ou had done that day, and possibly how tired she was from doing such incredible magic.

Gan Ou gratefully sat down, acknowledging the privilege of being allowed to speak before the elders while seated with a bow of her head.

"I lost someone today," she started off with. "No, I lost too many good people today. The direction to attack the priests was correct, but it came at such a high cost, as they are well defended." Gan Ou took a deep breath. "The grief and the rage—it was all too much. I called up the winds that I knew lived deep inside me. And they answered me for the first time."

Hi Lop nodded. "We all have lost far too many people," she said quietly. "And we cannot all become great heroes, the new legends of our time. Do you think, though, that you might be able to teach others to call the winds?"

Gan Ou shrugged. She'd been thinking about that earlier, when she'd finally rested enough that she could form thoughts and perhaps even full sentences again. "I can try," she said. "When I went through the wall formed by the Bone People, I felt the hole where the winds lived." She paused, trying to sort out her tired thoughts. "I think, I think only the others who feel such a hole can be taught. Should even try."

Hi Lop nodded, then gave her a sly grin. "In other words, we shouldn't waste your time by making you try to teach everyone."

Gan Ou couldn't help but give a tired snort of laughter. "Yes, exactly. It isn't the ones who want it who will be able to learn. It's only those who can find the place where the magic should go." She couldn't help but yawn, though she tried to contain it.

"Rest," Hi Lop said. "In the morning, we will begin."

Gan Ou paused before she pushed herself up. She knew she'd been dismissed. But she still had to ask.

"Did it make a difference?" Gan Ou said. "Did we win, finally?"

Hi Lop paused, then cautiously nodded. "We did. We held the field. But as you said, at such a cost."

Gan Ou sighed, then rose, and tottered out of the tent. Two of her cohort stepped forward immediately, grasping her arms, helping her limp away.

"What did they want?" Pan Su asked in a quiet whisper.

"They want me to teach," Gan Ou said. "Help the Wind People find their winds."

It was a terrible duty. Gan Ou recognized that she would be responsible for killing so many of the Bone People now, not necessarily directly but indirectly.

She would be one of the few who could do it. Before the war had started, she was one of the very few of the Wind People who'd killed another person, though it had been so long ago and resulted in her banishment.

In the end, her guilt over causing so many deaths would be worth it.

Or at least that was what she told herself. She hadn't come back from her banishment just to lose her home.

GAN OU STARTED the next morning. Fifty people were to be her first students.

It surprised her that the elder Ru Jing, the boy she'd fought over and had killed for so long ago, was one of them.

Or maybe he'd just come to watch over her, sent by the

elders. He still looked at her sourly. Much of his handsomeness had been stolen by time, giving him more of a grim look. Or maybe that had just been the war.

Clouds covered the sky that morning and fog misted the ground, making the world seem softer, wrapped in gray blankets. It would burn off soon enough, and Gan Ou would have to face the searing light of day. The elders had let Gan Ou know that she had two days in which to teach other Wind People everything she could. This was only the first group of students. She'd have others later that afternoon.

And hopefully by then, more teachers to help spread her lessons.

Luckily, her students that morning had all listened to the elders. They all claimed to feel the same hole that she'd felt.

Gan Ou didn't bother explaining that the winds she'd found hadn't completely filled that space. There was more she could do, would do, once circumstances forced her hand.

While not good at giving speeches, Gan Ou found she could still speak well enough from the heart, directing those who listened to find their rage and grief.

The winds listened to their hearts, not their words.

Maybe one in ten could manage the sorts of winds necessary to kill someone. However, most of those she taught could raise some wind, though frequently it wouldn't be useful for anything other than sweeping the floor or blowing leaves out of a house. Ru Jing was one of the latter, which gave Gan Ou a petty thrill.

She'd ended the second day with twenty-four who could direct serious winds, though none of them appeared to have her strength. Maybe it would come with battle. Or maybe it would only come with stubborn age.

The elders devised plans for how to deploy the Wind mages—not a term that Gan Ou had invented, but one she accepted.

While Gan Ou taught, others experimented. Could they take on a partial animal form like Lan Gi had in the myths? Could the winds carry news from far away? What else could they do with the winds, what other magic might they acquire?

And would any of it be enough to turn the tide and finally push the Bone People back?

———

THE ELDERS HAD WISELY DECIDED that they would not be able to hide these new abilities from the Bone People. They couldn't depend on surprise in their plans.

The two armies met on the same field. That hadn't happened often—generally the Bone People would take the field, pushing the Wind People back. No grass remained in the field, just cold mud that would stick in her paws. The clouds had disappeared, leaving the day clear and bright, as if this was just another almost-spring day. It didn't feel appropriate for the work ahead, but Gan Ou knew she couldn't change the weather with her new powers, as much as she might like.

While the Wind People had come up with new tactics, the elders had warned that the Bone People were sure to have developed new attacks themselves, and to be on the lookout for such things.

One of the elders had postulated that magic begat magic. As the Wind People found their magic, and brought more of it to the field, the Bone People would be able to do the same. Possibly this was why the Wind People had allowed the magic to flow away from them, as the need for doing terrible things had diminished.

None of the Wind People stayed in human form. They planned on transforming once they got into place.

Gan Ou was in her favorite wolf form. There were too many wolves and bears for the Bone People to be able to target her that day. Many had voluntarily taken the same form to help provide cover, which warmed her heart as well as made her feel slightly uncomfortable with all the attention.

Great winds suddenly howled across the open space between the two armies, pushing at the line of Bone People, then carrying back the scent of their fear.

Good.

Gan Ou growled deeply in her chest. So did those standing around her. A solid wall of animal noises spread across the open, muddy field, guaranteed to raise the hackles of all those who heard.

Some signal that Gan Ou missed sent the two armies surging forward.

This time, the Wind People split into several smaller groups just before they engaged the enemy, shrinking down to much smaller animals. They dove behind the enemy line, pushing back as far as they could on their initial run before transforming again, growing in size, regaining their teeth and claws.

The priests, as predicted, had stayed further behind this time. They knew they were now targets.

Gan Ou had discovered that she needed to see the person she was sending her winds against. She couldn't just find the scent of a priest and attack him. Like the other Wind mages, she frequently conjured false winds, blowing this way and that, to confuse the priests and to drive fear into the hearts of their warriors.

When Gan Ou finally spotted her first prey, she sent her warriors forward to distract him before she picked him up with her winds.

That was when she discovered the new attack of the Bone priests.

Large bones, each wider than the width of her palm, suddenly pushed their way out of the earth. They curved as they shot up, surrounding her. The edges were razor sharp and sliced the side of her leg. The bones grew fast and tall, far above her head, and formed a perfect sphere, trapping her inside. She instantly felt tired, her magic being sapped from her.

The cage started growing smaller. It would cut her to ribbons quickly if she didn't get out.

Gan Ou's winds could tear apart the cage, or she could use them to tear apart the priest.

She chose the damned priest.

He was a scrawny man, tough and wiry. His look of triumph made her even angrier.

Stupid priest was *not* about to win.

He wore stronger bone armor than what Gan Ou had encountered before, her winds slipping off when she tried grabbing his arms or legs.

Damn it! She had to kill him. Quickly before her prison killed her. The bones surrounding her were mere inches from touching her.

Gan Ou wrapped one wind around the priest's body, holding him still. Then she formed hands out of a second, grabbing hold of his head.

Then she gave a quick snap, forcing the two winds into opposite directions abruptly.

The head of the priest suddenly lolled to the side. The body dropped like a sack of bones.

The bones containing her stopped shrinking.

Gan Ou found herself shaking. Damn it. That had been too close.

She sent the words *duck down!* before she sent her winds to smash the structure. Pieces of sharp bone flew everywhere, slicing everything they encountered.

Tiny shards imbedded themselves in her skin, pinpricks of fire everywhere. She quickly transformed herself back into a wolf, pushing the slivers out of her skin as fur grew there instead.

She'd have to find another way to destroy the cursed bone prisons.

Next time.

BY THE END of the day, the Wind People had firmly taken the field, pushing the Bone People back. Only two of the Wind magicians had been slain, though all had been injured to a greater or lesser extent.

It was their first decisive victory.

Celebrations sprang up at many of the individual campfires across the plain, people laughing and dancing as they celebrated.

Still others took the time to more properly mourn, allowing themselves to feel the sorrow they'd kept bottled up.

Other magics had been discovered in the face of the battle that day, not just stronger winds but calling the leaves and twigs as well, forming clouds of dust to envelop the priests.

Gan Ou understood that this was just a start. Merely winning a battle didn't mean that they'd won the war. The Bone People had more tricks up their sleeve.

More of her people were going to die.

It was up to her to make damned sure that more of the Bone People did as well.

How her people would recover from the war, how they would bottle up such terrible deeds, would be up to the elders.

Chapter Two

STONE

NOALANON SLOWLY CAME BACK to zirself. Ze recognized that time had passed. How much, ze wasn't certain.

But morning had come and ze was sitting at the table with Jolapen and their three children, Kalepef, Turkastein, and Mathigorn. They were all eating their minerals. A bowl sat in front of zir. Ze had been slowly feeding zirself. The children were all dressed, ready for school, while Jolapen had on one of zir nicer work shirts. Noalanon sat looking at the quiet comfort of home as ze felt zir soul settle in.

With a start, Noalanon stared at the children. When had they gotten so big? How much time had ze passed in dreams? Mathigorn, the youngest, had always been seven going on seventeen. But the twins, too, seemed to hold themselves with a maturity ze hadn't seen before.

Even though Noalanon could see that they sat together at the table in the front room, the polished stone cold under zir palms, the light over the table golden and warm, there was still a wall of glass between zir and the world. The words of the twins came through distorted, as if they spoke underwater.

Noalanon turned zir head to look at Jolapen. Ah, zir mate. Ze felt…something tugging at zir. Some undercurrent, beneath the glass.

Jolapen turned zir focus away from their youngest, Mathigorn, to Noalanon, their eyes meeting.

When had Jolapen gone so pale? Zir skin used to be a dark gray color, like wet slate. Now, it almost had a powdery coating to it, as though it had been covered in fine ashes. Like ze had aged too, grown brittle and old.

"Noalanon?" Jolapen said.

Noalanon read the words on zir lips rather than heard them with zir ears. Ze blinked. Ze found ze could do that. Ze then nodded. There. Ze could do that as well. There was still too big of a gap to reach across for zir to form words, though.

The children had grown still as stones, as if they were frightened. Noalanon wanted to reassure them, but that barrier was too solid.

"Oh, thank the gods," Jolapen said. Ze slid zir hand over the table and wrapped it around Noalanon's cold hand. "I knew you were still there."

Or at least that was what Noalanon thought ze said. The words were still hard to hear.

"Warm up your Mana!" Jolapen directed.

Suddenly, the children all pressed against Noalanon. The sudden warmth surprised zir.

Why was ze so cold? Ze reached for zir own internal controls. Surely ze could warm zirself.

Why were they so hard to reach? How could they be broken? Did ze need to see a healer? Have someone prescribe a different combination of minerals?

Noalanon let the external world disappear as ze focused on zirself. Something was wrong with zir.

Time passed. Noalanon found zirself drifting again.

No, wait. Ze had something to do.

Again, ze focused on zir internal temperature. Ze wasn't cold. Ze couldn't be cold. All ze had to do was to raise zir own internal temperature.

There. That was how.

It was as if ze had forgotten. As if the barrier had come between zir and zirself.

Noalanon found zirself taking a deep breath, feeling zir lungs expand, as if ze hadn't breathed good air in a long, long time. Warmth slowly radiated from zir core, warming zir extremities. Ze blinked, and found zirself looking out of zir eyes again.

"Noalanon?"

Ze sat on the couch in the living room with Jolapen. Zir mate held zir hand.

Noalanon nodded. The wall of glass had thinned considerably since the last time, since breakfast…that morning? Some other morning? Ze still didn't know how much time had passed.

Jolapen's voice was almost normal. The world had mostly returned. The couch softly supported zir, and ze could smell the bright yellow daffodils that stood in a vase on the low table in front of them.

They were zir favorite flower. Jolapen must have gotten them for zir.

Noalanon cleared zir throat. It had been a while since ze had spoken, ze could tell that.

"What…what happened?" Noalanon said, forcing the words out. Zir voice was harsh and broken, rough rocks grating together.

Jolapen's eyes grew wide. "You're here!" ze exclaimed. "You're really here!"

Noalanon wasn't sure what Jolapen meant by that. But ze

nodded.

Tears formed in Jolapen's eyes. Noalanon reached up and brushed at them with zir thumb. Then ze drew Jolapen close, sharing a kiss that went on and on, warming zir all the way back up.

Ze found zirself crying as well, holding Jolapen close and rocking back and forth on the couch.

Suddenly, the bubble around Noalanon popped. The world came rushing back into focus. Ze couldn't help but gasp.

Jolapen pulled back abruptly. "What is it?" ze asked, searching Noalanon's face intently.

Noalanon understood Jolapen's concern now. "I'm here," Noalanon said. "The world is here. I can hear clearly." Ze swallowed. "Taste. Touch. Feel." Tears welled up in zir eyes again. It all seemed like too much suddenly. "What happened?" ze still made zirself ask.

Jolapen tenderly embraced zir. Noalanon reveled in the warmth. "I've been so cold," Noalanon confessed. "Why?"

"It was the Bone People," Jolapen said. "Those damned priests did something to you. How much do you remember?"

Noalanon gasped. "We brought the king here! Their stupid, rotten king!" She remembered how Forni had fooled them.

That was also the last thing that ze remembered.

Jolapen sighed. "Yes, you were tricked. Then the priests did something to you. They broke you, somehow. You were no longer there. Your body still worked. You would do anything I asked of you. But your soul was missing."

"Forni learned that we could resist the priests by adjusting our internal temperature," Noalanon said. "They figured out how to overwhelm those controls."

"I knew that there was something wrong with your temperature," Jolapen said. "You were always cold. I first noticed that you started to wake up when you were warmer. So I tried to keep you warm. Both I and the children."

Noalanon shuddered. She remembered that one time when she'd started coming back. At the breakfast table with the children. How they'd all looked scared. And so much older. It must have been hard on them, dealing with a Mana who wasn't really there.

"How long has it been?" Noalanon asked. Ze had to know. "How long was I…gone?"

"Almost four weeks," Jolapen said. "But you're back now." Ze drew Noalanon closer, pulled zir to zir chest. "I missed you so much."

Noalanon clung to zir mate. Ze reached for that bedrock connection that they'd shared while ze had been traveling.

A river of warmth poured into Noalanon's soul. Yes, this was what ze needed, what ze had been lacking. It was also what had brought zir back.

Jolapen appeared to relax suddenly. "You're really here," ze whispered.

"I am," Noalanon said. Or thought ze said. Ze couldn't be sure what words came out with zir voice and what was just shared now.

The pair of them floated in blissful connection, each complete with the soul light of the other bathing them.

Finally, Noalanon surfaced. "Where are the children?" ze asked, looking around.

"They're at school," Jolapen said. "You have been 'waking' more every day for the past week. So I took a chance and didn't go in to work today in order to be with you, in case you woke further today. I didn't want you to be alone when you came back."

"Thank you," Noalanon said. "You brought me back," ze added, tenderly reaching up to caress zir face.

Jolapen nodded, then sighed. "We're going to have to figure out how to keep you here."

"What do you mean?" Noalanon said. Ze withdrew, suddenly cold again. The world battered at zir senses, everything overwhelming again.

"The damned priests come and visit you every night," Jolapen said. "They send that black filth over you, trying to keep you contained. The children and I have managed to keep ourselves free so far. Most of the Stone People do, actually. But some feel it's just a matter of time before we all lose our wills to them."

"How far have they gotten on that tower of theirs?" Noalanon asked.

"It's been completed for a couple of weeks now," Jolapen said. "They use it once a week to 'pray' over all our souls, spreading their filth and control."

"We've got to stop them," Noalanon said.

Jolapen gave zir a look.

"What?"

"Now, I know you're truly back," Jolapen said with a grin. "There's a great injustice being done. And you're going to stop it."

NOALANON FOUND that it was easier than ze had expected to remain frozen in fear and appear dull when the knock on their door came that evening. At least it was later that night, after the children had all been sent to their beds.

Jolapen gave Noalanon a warning squeeze on zir arm before ze went to answer the frightening summons.

Three of the damned Bone priests came into their house. They didn't even have the courtesy of wiping their boots off before they stomped across zir clean slate floor.

They wore ash on their faces. It smelled bitter to zir, as if they'd mixed it with acrid soil. Black lines had been added around their eyes to make them seem larger, as well as streaks across their cheeks. They were shorter than Jolapen, but ze stooped zir head a little, so it wasn't as obvious.

"You missed work today," the one in the middle accused Jolapen.

Noalanon tagged him as the most important of the three, based on the fanciness of the belt he wore.

Jolapen came and sat beside Noalanon again. Ze took zir hand—ze must have always done that, every time the damned priests came.

Noalanon had to remind zirself not to raise the temperature of zir hand to match Jolapen's, though that was what ze wanted to do as soon as they touched.

Then Jolapen let go of zir hand, maybe realizing the internal struggle going in inside Noalanon.

"I was worried about Noalanon," Jolapen said honestly. "You know how ze has been. I was hoping…"

"She remains lost?" the main priest asked.

Again, Noalanon had to remember to breathe and be still, and not to react. How dare this priest assume that ze was female? That angered zir as much as anything else.

"Ze does," Jolapen lied, zir head dropping.

Only Noalanon saw the smile the priests gave at that.

"Let us see if we can help heal her," the priest said, stepping forward.

Familiar blackness swirled out from the priests. Noalanon felt it settle on zir skin. It surprised zir that ze didn't find it as disgusting as ze once had, the first time ze had encountered it. Not that ze welcomed it. But ze could understand how some people would grow used to it.

Then the darkness pushed its way into zir body. Ze tried to focus on the coolness of the table under zir hands and not gag. The icky inkiness was seeking out zir internal controls, trying to wrap them in ashes and dirt.

This time, Noalanon resisted. Ze poured out zir internal heat, keeping it wrapped tightly around zir core and not letting it creep out to zir extremities. The awful numbness that came with the blackness burned out quickly.

The priest intoned his prayer to his god Valtyr, asking for him to save this poor soul, to bring her fully into the darkness, to send his healing strength to her.

The arrogance and the stupid priest's gendering made Noalanon grit zir teeth harder.

Resisting the darkness pouring out from the priest was much easier than Noalanon had expected. Or else the priest wasn't really trying. The prayer seemed short to Noalanon, though ze didn't really have anything to compare it to.

Once the priest was finished, he walked forward and touched Noalanon's hand.

It was still cool to the touch.

Noalanon stilled zirself for a closer examination, for the priest to look into zir eyes or touch zir face.

But he seemed satisfied, and left abruptly.

Noalanon sat in silence for a moment, holding up zir hand to make sure that Jolapen stayed quiet as well. Noalanon didn't speak until after ze was certain that ze heard the closing of the front gate, that the priests had actually left the premises.

"May the gods damn each and every one of them," Noalanon said through gritted teeth. "May they never be reborn in Ishkra's love. May their souls be wiped off the blessed firmament, never to return."

Jolapen gave zir a crooked smile. "Tell me how you really feel."

Noalanon tried to contain zir anger. "They've been coming in every day and doing that?" ze asked.

"They have. I'm glad that their work has been unsuccessful," Jolapen said reaching across the table to take Noalanon's hand.

Noalanon gratefully raised the temperature in zir extremities, enjoying how Jolapen smiled when ze felt zir warmth returning.

"The priest's work has been successful. Just not how they've imagined," Noalanon said, squeezing zir partner's hand tightly. "I seem to have developed more of an immunity. I understand now how that damned darkness of theirs is working."

"Really?" Jolapen said, blinking, surprised. "That's wonderful!" ze added, leaning over and kissing Noalanon. "I'm so glad."

Noalanon knew that Jolapen had been very worried that the priests and their prayers would take zir away from zir again. Ze wrapped zir arms around Jolapen and held zir partner close as Jolapen cried, zir relief palpable.

"I'm back. I'm here," Noalanon said, kissing Jolapen's head.

When Jolapen had managed to compose zirself, ze looked back up at Noalanon. "I know you're here. At least for now. But you won't stay."

"How can I?" Noalanon asked. "Do you want this filth to spread to our children? For them to always live in fear? No, we have to get rid of the Bone People once and for all."

"But how?" Jolapen asked.

"You said that Sugaoshi had been organizing people, before she was taken inside the temple," Noalanon said. "That ze had been building an army of resisters. That they had plans to attack, just before ze was taken."

"Yes," Jolapen said slowly, nodding zir head. "But I don't know who Sugaoshi had been in contact with. If all of those people are still safe, or if they'd report us."

Noalanon shook zir head. "They're still safe. They wouldn't have been corrupted so easily again. But we need to find out who they are. We need to organize that attack again. We need Sugaoshi," Noalanon said. "We must free zir."

"The priests won't let zir go," Jolapen said, grimacing. "The council asked once, formally, and were told that since the priests were making such good progress at 'healing' Sugaoshi, they didn't think it was healthy for zir to go home yet. They promised they would release zir soon."

"That means that they haven't fully stripped Sugaoshi's will from zir," Noalanon said. "It means we can save zir."

"I agree with your logic," Jolapen said slowly. "The stupid priests won't release Sugaoshi until ze is as brainless as you were."

Noalanon shuddered. Ze didn't like to think about how the priests were torturing Sugaoshi, tucked away in their temple.

Sugaoshi had had a plan, though. Had already put into place the means of attack, for tearing down the temple.

The choice was between starting over from scratch, or rescuing Sugaoshi.

While Noalanon loved zir partner and zir people, this was a battle they were facing. The Stone People were slow to move, as well as slow to anger.

They needed Sugaoshi and zir anger in order to defeat the Bone People.

And Noalanon had a good idea of how to free the former councilmember.

NOALANON STEPPED OUTSIDE of their home and paused, the night pressing in against zir. The Stone People had never bothered with stringing lights outside of their houses or in their yards. They could see just fine in the dark, better than all the other Peoples, including the Bone People.

It took a moment for Noalanon's eyes to readjust to the dimness. Or at least that was what ze told zirself. It wasn't that ze suddenly felt all the world around zir instead of being in a closed, safe space. Ze hadn't suddenly stepped out in the wild. This was zir city. Ze was safe.

Noalanon took one deep breath, then another, calming zirself, smelling the fresh air that carried the smell of sweet spring flowers. Ze pushed zir senses down into the ground, feeling the solid earth supporting zir. The fear tasted bitter in zir mouth and ze swallowed, trying to dispel it.

Ze was in the land of the Stone People. Everything would be easier here than in the land of the Wind People. Ze had to remind zirself of that. Plus, ze had full control of zirself. The damned priests wouldn't be able to overwhelm zir again.

There. It took zir a few moments to find the solid earth under zir feet again, to draw up the magic of zir homeland. It rose up zir legs like sinking into comforting wet clay, caressing zir skin and supporting zir weight fully.

The priests had stripped that feeling all away from zir.

Ze found zirself grinding zir teeth in anger. Damn them. Damn them all.

Jolapen remained just inside the doorway, looking out. "Are you all right?" ze whispered.

Noalanon nodded. "Just finding my feet again."

They'd argued about it, but in the end, Jolapen had agreed to stay home with the children. If Noalanon was caught, Jolapen could claim innocence, that Noalanon had wandered away from their home without zir knowledge, that ze had no idea what zir mate had been up to.

They had to protect the children at all costs. And truthfully, Jolapen had very little idea of what Noalanon would do that evening.

After one last deep breath, Noalanon marched forward, out of the gate and onto the solid stone sidewalk. Both it and the dirt-filled street just past it were sadly empty. As ze walked, ze saw two People scurry down the street, into their homes, as if afraid to be caught out after dark.

That was just one more thing that ze was determined to change. Killapany used to be alive at all hours.

And it would be again.

Fortunately, the Bone People had built their temple close to the main market. They'd taken out a block of warehouses for their arrogant structure. They'd built on the eastern side of the market, because the east, their homeland, was important to them. If they'd been thinking, they might have tried placing it on the southern side, in the direction of the holy mountain.

They didn't understand that location also made them more vulnerable. The marketplace was an easy place for many people to gather, all with a good excuse.

Maybe not so much at night, but during the day, many different people visited the marketplace. Artists, teachers, merchants, builders. And miners.

After Noalanon had come back to zirself, Jolapen had notified Juhala that the councilmember might want to come and visit. At that meeting, Juhala had put Noalanon in touch with the other rebels. While the councilmember adamantly didn't want to be involved with their plans—ze was in too vulnerable of a position—ze could at least introduce the right people to each other.

In twos or threes, the other rebels had come to Noalanon's house over the past few weeks, supposedly looking in on zir in zir poor witless state. Tonight, the group was putting the final phase into place, with Noalanon coming out for the first time to see what it was they'd done. While ze had some idea, ze hadn't been told everything. The damned priests still came to pray over zir every night, and the others were worried that ze might be compromised.

The northern side of the market square had a few shops with large warehouses built into the back of them. Plus the ice house.

Merchants and their assistants constantly went in and out of the entrance to the ice house. As did many others.

While it was possible for the Stone People to both heat as well as chill rocks with their hands, sometimes ice was more appropriate. They also needed it for preserving food for the other Peoples. Much of the ice in the ice house came from the previous winter, chopped out of frozen lakes, carried into the city, and placed underground. The merchants in charge of the icehouse spent their time keeping the walls chilled and the air clean, so the ice stayed fresh.

From the icehouse, it was easy for the Stone People to tunnel out, under the market place, toward the temple of the Bone People. They knew the layout of the temple, as their own builders had created it.

None of the temple lay underground. Everything was above ground. The Bone People hadn't thought to dig down.

They probably hadn't realized how easy it was for the Stone People to do so. That now worked in the rebels' favor.

Noalanon slipped through the quiet streets, mourning the teashops that were closed, the playhouses and reading rooms. Though the air smelled fresh and good, she still missed the scents of the city. The Bone People had cut off a good portion of the life that the Stone People had by not allowing them to gather at night.

It could all be brought back. The city could live again. Or at least Noalanon told zirself that.

No one had gathered in the marketplace, either. Normally, there would be at least a few little stands open, serving tea, with some live music playing. Instead, it felt like a ghost town, a place where spirits rejected by Ishkra gathered. It made shivers run down Noalanon's spine.

Noalanon stuck close to the darkened buildings, making zirway toward the ice house. Ze walked silently, the soft winds making more noise. The pungent odor of fresh leather goods wafted out from the warehouse she passed. Ze drew zir strength from the solid stone beneath zir, supporting zir muscles even though ze hadn't walked so far in over a month.

Ze suddenly heard the sound of many feet, walking. It was the sound of the Bone People's guards approaching.

Fear spiked through Noalanon. Ze froze, becoming like stone, barely breathing.

The large group passed in front of Noalanon on a cross street. They walked loudly down the center of the street, carrying lanterns hanging on poles.

Didn't they understand that the light and the noise just made them an easier target?

But only if they were afraid of attack. Which they weren't.

Noalanon couldn't wait to teach them fear.

After the guards had passed, Noalanon darted quickly across the street, then slid carefully up to the door of the icehouse. It was locked. Ze knocked, the sound loud in the quiet street, then whispered the password.

Would they let zir in?

Finally, the door cracked open. Noalanon gratefully slipped inside, happy to get off the street.

The room Noalanon stepped into was small and felt cramped after being outside. No lights were on inside—Stone People saw well enough, even in a dark enclosed space. A single desk took up the middle of the space, an effective barrier, discouraging anyone from walking further into the building. During the day, one of the ice merchants sat behind the desk, taking orders. A long bench was shoved up against the far wall, empty now but normally full of runners, eager to go down the stairs into the icehouse below to gather the ice, then to carry it up and to the appropriate place in the market.

To Noalanon's right stood a short, squat Stone Person. Despite the dark, Noalanon still turned zir face toward the other person so that ze could see zir better.

The person in front of Noalanon said quietly, "We're so glad that you're here."

It took Noalanon a moment to place the voice of Hirshamin. Ze hadn't been told the names of the other rebels.

"You're awake!" Noalanon said gleefully. Ze reached out and grasped arms with the builder.

"Woke before you did," Hirshamin growled. "My children brought me back," ze added after a moment.

Noalanon nodded, remembering that Hirshamin had born a remarkable number of children, including two sets of twins, if ze was recalling correctly.

"It was my partner, Jolapen, who was there for me," Noalanon said.

"That appears to be the case with all of us," Hirshamin said. "Our relationships, our connections, were able to bring us out of the darkness."

"Have you heard from Yunaki?" Noalanon asked. Jolapen had thought that both of zir traveling companions were still lost.

"No," Hirshamin said. "As far as I know, Yunaki is still witless."

Noalanon sighed. Hopefully Yunaki could be brought back. Ze hadn't had a mate or children, though. Ze had been a teacher, like most of the Stone People who'd traveled to the lands of the Wind People. Maybe zir students could help…

That was a problem for another day.

Noalanon followed Hirshamin into the back room, which only contained a set of steep stone stairs leading down into the ice room below. Light blossomed from the wide opening in the floor, welcome and cheery.

Cold flowed out of the hole in the floor as well. Noalanon automatically adjusted zir inner temperature in the face of it. Though ze made adjustments to zir temperature without thinking about it, ze still noticed frequently after the fact. It always pleased zir that ze had that skill, as well as pissed zir off that the ability had been stolen from zir.

Hirshamin walked down the steep stairs first. Noalanon followed, taking zir time and stepping carefully, leaning back so ze wouldn't fall face first onto the dirt floor below.

The air smelled of the fresh straw that covered the blocks of ice stacked high against the wall. Noalanon could see zir breath as ze walked along the precise path between the stacks, following Hirshamin.

The ice room was huge, particularly compared to the tiny office above, being half a block long as well as that wide. On the far wall, kitty-corner from the staircase, a large black hole gaped.

Noalanon quickly followed Hirshamin over to the entrance of what turned out to be a tunnel that stood over six feet tall but only half again as wide. The walls of the tunnel had been left rough, as if it had been dug in a hurry. More lights lit the way inside, cheap lamps filled with glowing rocks. The smell of straw and ice gave way to the scent of good dirt.

"We've already tunneled our way under the temple," Hirshamin told Noalanon. "We think we've identified the room where they're keeping Sugaoshi and the others."

"There are others?" Noalanon asked, appalled. How dare they keep any of zir people imprisoned?

Hirshamin nodded grimly. "Yes. Maybe half a dozen or

so. Or at least that's our best estimate, based on the amount of minerals that the Bone People need on a regular basis."

That was a clever way to count noses, Noalanon had to admit. "I bet they're starved, then."

"Yes, that is our guess as well. They're being fed a basic diet. Nothing specialized. They're likely to be weak."

"We'll carry them out if we have to," Noalanon said.

"Aye, we will," Hirshamin assured zir. "I've got some strong people at the other end. We were just waiting for you."

"You should have just moved forward!" Noalanon chided. Ze didn't want anyone to have to stay in the gentle "care" of the Bone People a moment longer than they needed to be.

Hirshamin shrugged. "You were the instigator, to get us this far," ze admitted. "Though I had been thinking along the same lines, once I came back."

Noalanon wasn't surprised. It made sense that those who had visited the Wind People would have the most forward momentum.

Hirshamin led the way through the rough tunnel. Noalanon could tell by the way the miner reached out and touched the walls now and again that the roughly carved state of the tunnel offended Hirshamin. It was solidly built— Noalanon was certain that many miners had been recruited for the task, if they had been able finish it in just three days —however, they hadn't taken the time to make it smooth and beautiful.

Over a dozen people waited in the area just under the temple—at least two for every prisoner, so it would be possible to carry them out if they weren't able to walk on their own.

One of their own priests was there. Ze carried dirt brought from the base of the holy mountain, sprinkling it on all of their heads in blessing. Noalanon didn't think that it would do any good. Only the sight of the holy mountain would help them clear their heads. Ze had missed that sight so much, though once ze had returned, ze had spent every day facing the direction of the mountain, sending thanks to Kiproary for zir guidance. It was zir one regret, coming out so late at night, not being able to see the mountain itself.

A set of crude stairs had been carved into the very end of the tunnel, leading upward toward the ceiling. Once the priest was finished, one of the miners climbed the stairs. Ze held a large prospector's hammer, which was about a foot wide. One side had a wicked spike on the end, for digging into and prying out rocks. The other side was flat and could be used for cracking stones apart.

Noalanon felt zir breath catch. Even if ze was captured again by the damned priests, ze would come back. Ze was too determined not to.

With a dull thud, the miner used the top of zir hammer to bash against the ceiling. The mighty blow caused a shower of smaller rocks. Noalanon raised zir arms to shield zir head. The air was suddenly hazy with dust.

Three more strikes, and the hammer punched through the ceiling and into the open air above.

For a moment, they all paused.

"Help us?" came a very quiet voice.

The miner went into frenzied action, tearing at the opening, making it wide enough so the Stone People could get through it and up to the top.

The growl that came from the first few People who went up was audible to all those standing below. One of the rescuers stuck zir head down and called for Hirshamin and Noalanon to come up.

Noalanon hurried up the stairs. Ze managed to contain zir gasp.

There were eight Stone People trapped in the room. They all wore iron bars that went between their ankles and wrists, that were then chained to the wall. None of the Stone People could stand on their own. The air smelled of stale rock, like a tomb. Lights burned in the corners, crude torches that had obviously been set there by the Bone People.

How many of the imprisoned Stone People were witless? Noalanon didn't have time to try to look. Ze understood why ze and Hirshamin had been called. They were the only ones who had any experience breaking the Bone People's chains.

Quickly, Noalanon knelt beside the first Stone Person, freezing the chain then striking it hard with the heel of zir hand.

Ze might have struck it too hard, as the iron shattered like ice, shards flying across the room. Noalanon took a deep breath, a sourness filtering in, like mold-covered wet earth.

Hirshamin started to help another person on the far side of the room. The same sharp crack of iron shattering filled the space.

Noalanon touched the iron bar that held the first Stone Person, but realized that it was much thicker than any of the chain loops, possibly a solid bar. "Leave the bars," ze said quietly to the others. The prisoners would just have to be carried out.

"Noalanon?" came a whisper from the last Stone Person in the line.

Noalanon looked up. It was Sugaoshi. Ze was difficult to recognize, as zir soft brown hair was matted and zir skin looked ashen instead of black. The pretty white jacket that ze had been wearing was filthy with long tears down the side.

"We're here to rescue you," Noalanon said firmly as ze broke the councilmember's chains.

The giggle that Sugaoshi gave made Noalanon pause and look at the other.

"I'm fine, really," Sugaoshi said. Ze still gasped when Noalanon pulled Sugaoshi up.

"What is it?" Noalanon asked.

Sugaoshi nodded toward zir side, where zir jacket was in shreds.

Long cuts had been made down the councilmember's side. Some were old, but some were recent. Blood still beaded along the edge of the freshest. Noalanon nearly gagged. The smell was worse than black mold rot, as it had a sweetness to it, like rotten apples.

"They were trying to find the best knives for cutting us," Sugaoshi said. Ze shivered. "The best weapons to kill us all."

Noalanon shook zir head in disbelief. Kill them all? Not just enslave them? Or merely kill the rebels? "We need your plans, how you were going to attack," ze said.

"The original plans won't work," Sugaoshi warned as ze started shuffling toward the opening.

Was that really the case? Or had Sugaoshi lost hope being stuck here for so long?

"It's all right. I have better ones, now," Sugaoshi said.

Noalanon felt zirself grinning, something feral and not at all welcoming.

Two of the other rescuers stood on either side of the opening. They carefully picked Sugaoshi up and handed zir down the stairs to the others waiting below.

Noalanon stood in the prison cell and looked around, satisfied. All the Stone People had been rescued. The guards outside (if there were any) hadn't heard them, even the loud breaking of the chains.

Now, to the next phase of zir plan.

Metal plates had been bolted into the walls and floors, with large loops forged in them that held the chains. Noalanon and the others pushed the plates halfway into the walls, causing the stone to grow up around them. They pushed the chains as well, making it appears as if the Stone People had actually escaped into the rock walls. They wiped the floor clear of any footprints. The miners assured them that they could make the floor where the tunnel entrance had been completely smooth.

The Bone People would have lost all their prisoners. And they wouldn't have a clue how they'd escaped.

In the morning, the Stone People would start their attack.

And the Bone People would learn true fear.

Chapter Three

SEA

BAYASETH FLOATED IN HER OFFICE. A half-empty globe of stimulating tea sat on her desk. She'd barely left her office since everything had blown up in her face. She still loved the formality of the place, the beautiful mosaic that took up most of the floor, the gorgeous pearls and stones encrusted in the walls. She was determined to stay here and enjoy every moment of it, despite how hard she was working, as she was well aware that it would all be taken from her too soon.

A messenger swam in, grasping the pole that now seemed to be permanently stationed in front of her desk. Bayaseth yawned and stretched, reaching for the globe and sucking down the rest of its contents before nodding, ready to face the next task.

"The water and current workers need more supplies," he stated blandly, listing off three difficult-to-grow seaweeds.

Bayaseth didn't grind her teeth together, though she knew the expense for such seaweed was astonishing. She also knew she couldn't negotiate. The water and current workers had performed miracles, driving the plague waters created by

Brodalesh out of the city, keeping their own waters clean. Only a few hundred had died, instead of a few thousand.

There was also a good chance that the water and current workers needed the expensive food. They were performing a lot of magic to keep the waters clean, and needed to replenish themselves. It wasn't that they were taking advantage of the situation to give themselves such delicacies. The few times that Bayaseth had visited their group, she'd been impressed at how hard they'd been working. They had set up shifts, so that the currents would be maintained all day and all night.

She authorized the expense, told the messenger to go meet with the purser for the temple and get the funds, then go to the marketplace to find the delicacies. "Be sure to bargain for the best price," Bayaseth told him.

He nodded and left. The bells tolled evening prayers outside. Bayaseth knew that she couldn't leave her office, not yet. There was still a line of messengers outside, all the things she had to deal with before she would be allowed any rest. Only to do it again the next day.

Bayaseth knew she couldn't complain. At least not out loud. Liseth had pointed out that Bayaseth had lost that right because all of her problems were of her own making.

It wasn't fair. The current crisis wasn't even Bayaseth's fault. Not really. That stupid plague bringer Brodalesh had screwed up. She was supposed to create a disease that targeted Sea People who stayed in their land form. But what she'd created had turned out to be the opposite—a plague that primarily affected those who stayed in their water form.

Liseth had been fooled at first, thinking that Brodalesh's plague had originally been targeted toward the Bone People. But Brodalesh's assistant had survived long enough to tell the full story.

Damn him. Damn everyone.

The only thing that had kept Bayaseth alive so far had been Jolash the explorer, and the new city that they'd been slowly building at the mouth of the Lossheen river to the south. As well as the various towns that they'd created up and down the coast, mostly as part of the supply chain for materials for the new southern capital.

If only it hadn't been a plague that had driven her people out of Sillboden! With the coming of the Bone People, Shiboleth had been slowly emptying. Bayaseth's big plans could have all taken shape, with her being hailed as the savior of their time.

Instead of her name being cursed with bringing so many to Ishkra before their time.

It surprised Bayaseth that it was Jolash the explorer who came swimming into her office next. Jolash wore more clothing than most, with a shirt that tied around her wrists and pants that went down to her ankles. Her skin was covered in sores and pock marks, which Bayaseth assumed had been caused by an old plague that Jolash had survived as a child.

There wasn't any way to completely clean the waters, just to break up the concentration of the plague waters in the immediate area. Then pray that the waters didn't find a way to recombine at some future date, killing off more People. Or possibly mutating, as plagues often did.

"It is good to see you," Bayaseth told Jolash. She actually meant it this time. Though the explorer was not as cultured or educated as the priestess, and they had very little in common, Jolash at least appeared to not blame Bayaseth for everything and didn't come into her office already angry.

"And you, my lady," Jolash said. She paused, looking at Bayaseth closely. "You look tired, my lady."

Bayaseth shrugged. "Tell me something I don't already know." She smiled to take the sting out of her words.

Jolash nodded. "The five towns between here and the new capital at Lossheen have been building up nicely," she said. "There's a lack of housing, of course. More people coming in than we can handle."

Bayaseth knew that. She'd sent as many supplies as she could down the trail, including the heavy weights that hunters sometimes used to keep themselves moored in place when out in the wild waters. Closer into shore, Sea People used something similar to hold them in place while they slept, as they had no beds or houses or proper sleeping nets.

"And?" Bayaseth asked, when Jolash paused. "I did ask you to tell me something new," she said as an attempt at keeping the conversation a little more lighthearted.

"It's nothing I'd put in a report," Jolash said cautiously. "But I wanted you to know that the Sea People, well, they're thriving. Sure, they complain about the lack of everything. But the few who arrived pregnant, well, they've all had multiple births."

"Really?" Bayaseth said, clicking her tongue, very surprised. "That is interesting." She had assumed that because of all the threats, as well as the disruption to their lives, that those who were pregnant would only have single births.

Like Liseth, Bayaseth had been concerned about how the population of the Sea People had been dwindling for the past few decades. The Sea People didn't live as long as the other people, and children frequently passed before they reached maturity.

"Why do you suppose that is?" Bayaseth asked.

Jolash sighed before she answered. "It's my theory that the Sea People need more space," she said. "Being all crowded together in a big city is unhealthy."

Bayaseth opened her mouth, then closed it again. Of course, that was how Jolash felt. She'd always felt that way. It was one of the reasons why she was an explorer. She preferred the wild areas, didn't feel as comfortable in civilized places.

And yet…it was possible that Jolash had a valid point. Maybe the Sea People did need more space. Maybe they needed to live in smaller towns rather than in a single big city. She knew that those who lived outside Shiboleth had always had more births than those who lived inside it.

"That *is* an interesting theory," Bayaseth finally said. "I will bring it up with the regents. Make sure that they follow this trend, see if there's some merit to it."

The smile that Jolash gave Bayaseth completely transformed her face. It wasn't that Jolash wasn't pretty. With her creamy blue-white skin and her wide eyes, she might be considered beautiful, if one could overlook her brash manner and the rest of her ruined skin.

But just then, Jolash appeared to shine with an inner light that made her quite stunning.

"Thank you, my lady," Jolash said sincerely. She pushed herself forward, drawing closer to the priestess. "I have always enjoyed working for you."

Bayaseth suddenly understood what Jolash was talking about. The next time Bayaseth talked with the regents might be the last time she would be in a position of power. They'd already started discussing her replacement, debating whether to move forward while they were still in such a time of crisis.

This might be the last time that she got to meet Jolash in her beautiful office. Because it would no longer be her office.

"I have enjoyed working with you as well," Bayaseth said. She mostly meant it. Jolash was at least efficient, even if she did step outside of her place often.

"Thank you," Jolash said. She held out her hand.

Bayaseth reached over her desk and took it. The palm of the explorer's hand felt rough in her own, while the creamy skin on the back of her hand felt incredibly soft. They held hands like sisters for a moment, smiling at each other.

With a final nod of her head, Jolash let go and swam out of Bayaseth's office.

Bayaseth reached for the strong tea on her desk, disappointed to find the globe empty. Maybe she should send one of the messengers to fetch her more.

Or maybe not. She did want to sleep later that evening. When she was finally allowed to leave her office and go sleep, at least for a short while.

With a smile plastered on her face, Bayaseth greeted the next messenger, turning her attention again to the task at hand, no matter how loudly she wanted to complain about the whole mess.

BAYASETH FLOATED before the six regents, Liseth next to her. She knew better than to think that Liseth was on her side, or would argue for her.

No, Liseth was here to ensure that Bayaseth's punishment was sufficient to satisfy her petty soul. Luckily for her, the Sea People rarely killed anyone—they would just be banished.

Generally, the regents met on land, in the beautiful chamber they had there, with golden walls and remarkable tapestries. However, with the coming of the Bone People, the regents met more often in the water, despite the plague.

Their sea chamber was not as sumptuous, even with the stunning mosaic of waves done in blue, green, and gold glass that swirled from the floor and halfway up the walls. The ceiling was painted a plain whitish blue, and few stones or pearls encrusted the upper walls. It looked unfinished to Bayaseth, though she knew that the decorations were supposed to honor both the sea as well as the land.

Still, this was probably the last time she'd ever see the inside of this room.

The gold-covered resting poles that the regents held onto were arranged in a circle, so that none floated at the "head" or considered themselves most important.

Regent Solangess recited Bayaseth's crimes. Bayaseth had never liked Regent Solangess—she had a fake piety that set Bayaseth's teeth on edge.

Given the satisfaction in Regent Solangess's voice, Bayaseth figured the dislike was mutual.

Then Regent Ruschyard recited the mitigating factors that should work in Bayaseth's defense. The fact that since she'd already established a line of towns up and down the coast allowed the Sea People to escape the plague that Bayaseth had unleashed, giving them a place to live. The regents had discounted her statement about the people thriving in smaller towns, though Liseth had at least listened. Plus Regent Ruschyard listed how Bayaseth had been working hard to make things right.

It wasn't enough. Bayaseth knew that before she'd passed through the door.

"It is the considered agreement of this council that you be stripped of your title," Regent Abrassis declared when there were no other arguments to be made for or against Bayaseth. "And banished from both the city of Sillboden as well as the city of Lossheen."

Bayaseth kept her click of surprise to herself. She had expected the first part, as well as the possible banishment from Sillboden. It made sense, though. If Lossheen was to become a great city, they wouldn't want her there either. She would be stuck in the smaller towns, scraping by with a largess from whatever temple would deal with her.

Temples were supposed to see to the basic needs of the

people when they fell on hard times. She, however, would be barely tolerated. She knew that already.

How would she survive? Like Liseth, she had no children, no mate. No one to take care of her. Her own parents were long deceased. Her older sister had given her a room, but had also made it clear that it was temporary.

However, the regents had already passed their sentence. Bayaseth didn't see any recourse. She'd taken the actions she had, done the best she could.

If only it had turned out differently.

The regents appeared to be waiting for Bayaseth to say something. Maybe to thank them for their largess. She considered just swimming out in silence.

That didn't feel right either. Instead, Bayaseth bowed her head once and said, "I have always served Ishkra to the best of my ability," she maintained.

Even if that ability had fallen far short of need this time.

Bayaseth turned and swam out of the regents' chamber, into the hallway beyond. She'd already moved all her personal belongings from her rooms in the temple—some dresses, scrolls of poetry, a beautifully carved statue of Ishkra. Her goods on the land had also been moved.

Liseth came with her. Bayaseth couldn't help but ask, "Are you here to make sure that I leave?"

Liseth shook her head. "No, there are guards assigned to do that." She gestured behind her where two large hunters floated.

They would be the ones who escorted Bayaseth to the edge of the city. Hopefully she could bargain with them, get them to allow her a little more time to organize her things. She already had a room rented down in the first town beyond Sillboden.

"Then what do you want?" Bayaseth said.

"I could still have you killed," Liseth commented. "The regents might even thank me for it."

Bayaseth couldn't hide her click of surprise. "Really?" she said. "What brought that on? We were sisters, once."

The bitter laugh that Liseth gave sent cold fingers down Bayaseth's spine. "No, we were never sisters. I was too arrogant, remember? Didn't think enough about the Sea People. I understand, now, that you were actually referring to yourself. You were the arrogant one. You were the one who wanted her name listed in history as the savior of our People."

"You don't need to worry about that now, do you?" Bayaseth said, starting to swim away. "Your name will be remembered for that."

Liseth gave a more gentle laugh this time as she came up beside Bayaseth. "No, it won't. Ajooless, perhaps. Or maybe Mayleth."

Bayaseth nodded. Some of those who had originally left with Ajooless had returned with wondrous stories of Mayleth looking through the eyes of a minnow to bring them news of the Bone People.

"So you would kill me for my arrogance?" Bayaseth asked. She should at least know why she was dying when the hunters came for her.

"No, the reason I don't kill you is because your death won't bring back those who have already died," Liseth said. "If I thought it might help, you'd already find yourself wriggling on the spear of a hunter."

Bayaseth found herself swallowing against a suddenly dry throat. It was an awful threat, as threats went, to find oneself dangling on a spear, slowly bleeding out, instead of a more graceful death.

"You are capable of doing great work," Liseth added seriously. "Don't go and wallow in self-pity. Don't complain.

Do what's set in front of you. And you won't find hunters crossing your threshold."

Bayaseth knew that Liseth was serious. The priestess would kill Bayaseth if she gave her a reason. "What if I'm not allowed?" Bayaseth asked. "You know that no one will really tolerate me."

Liseth gave her a sharp smile. "That's your problem. But I'm sure that you'll find your own current. You always do."

A small group of Sea People floated up ahead. They appeared to be waiting for the pair of them.

"I wish you Ishkra's deep waters and solace in your darkest hours," Liseth said seriously as she paused. Then she reached out her hand.

Bayaseth paused, but then slowly reached across the space, taking Liseth's hand in her own and squeezing tightly for a moment.

"We were sisters, once," Liseth whispered. "Goodbye," she said out loud, letting go of Bayaseth's hand and swimming away.

Bayaseth hung her head for a moment. She wasn't in her land form. She couldn't take a deep breath. She gave herself a slight shake instead, refreshing the water all around her.

Her future awaited.

She looked up as the group of figures approached, assuming that it would be more guards.

Instead, Jolash and some of her crew swam up.

"Liseth asked that I help get you settled my lady, at least at the start," Jolash said.

Bayaseth was shocked that of all the people Liseth could have reached out to, she would find the explorer.

"But why?" Bayaseth asked, feeling as though all the currents around her had suddenly switched direction.

Jolash shrugged, obviously not wanting to say more.

Particularly in front of the guards now looming behind Bayaseth.

"Thank you," Bayaseth said, reaching out for Jolash's hard hand. The explorer had always been an outsider, her skin condition and her lack of education placing her firmly beneath the priestess.

Maybe Liseth had chosen wisely. Maybe Jolash could teach Bayaseth how to survive on the edges.

But only if Bayaseth in her arrogance would learn.

Bayaseth honestly hadn't known if she would live out the year.

For the first time since the regents had discovered her role behind the plague, she had hope that she might.

Chapter Four

WIND

KA LEM DREAMED OF DANCING. He wasn't like a whirlwind, flying in circles. No, he danced like the bear deep inside of him did, with her feet barely shuffling in place.

He danced before the gods in his dream. Sune Li appeared as a mighty fire, the light and sparks dancing with Ka Lem, encouraging him. Kiproary stood solid and firm, a mountainous dark being who neither smiled nor frowned, but remained neutral. Ishkra looked like a waterfall, but she sang cheerily as the water poured down, the loud splashing keeping time with Ka Lem's feet.

Valtyr was there too, triangular in shape, looking like a piece of night ripped from the sky, his edges rippling. Though the dark god stood apart from the others, Ka Lem had the feeling the god belonged there. Valtyr emanated a cold darkness that balanced out the heat and light from Sune Li and the others.

Who were the other beings who appeared before Ka Lem? He couldn't say for certain. More gods? Unknown ones? Or gods who had been forgotten? A watery form stood with the other gods, built out of slender reeds and mist. As well as a birdlike being, maybe a heron or a crane, with great stalklike legs. More stood in a line going either direction, their forms faded and misty.

Ka Lem found it difficult to dance. His limbs kept weighing him down and his mind wandered, his attention flickering in and out, buzzing like a slow firefly. The smell of sage burning woke him a little, as did the occasional cool splash of water from Ishkra.

He had to keep dancing. That much he knew. Or the darkness he danced above would take him.

It surprised him that the darkness that flowed around his feet was separate from Valtyr, who the Bone People worshipped as the god of the abyss.

However, the abyss was not from Valtyr. It was part of another force, a different, malevolent being, who nibbled at Ka Lem's life when his attention wandered and he forgot to keep shuffling his feet. It wasn't a god, but rather the antithesis of a god, as all the gods, those known and unknown, were part of creation, the natural cycle of life and death.

This dark being only knew destruction and chaos.

Even as Ka Lem found his consciousness rising, all the way up to waking, he found that he still needed to dance if he wanted to stay alive.

The Bone People had been preparing him for their great ceremony for weeks now, when the priests would take his life and enslave the souls of all of the Wind People. While they'd prayed over him constantly, they'd stopped trying to sap his will from him. That had been an improvement.

Then they reached the capital city of Melefels. Ka Lem hadn't spent much time traveling through the city before they'd arrived at their final destination. The poverty of the neighborhoods hadn't surprised him, given how abysmal their souls appeared to be.

The priests had taken Ka Lem off the back of the cart, allowing him to stand and walk around the large tent he was now enclosed in. Then they'd started to feed him herbs and concoctions that drained away his wits. They took the chains off his legs, but he couldn't focus enough to change shape and escape.

Ka Lem could tell that the Bone People were building up for the ceremony by the number of priests he saw regularly. They were constantly chanting, though they were no longer directing their prayers at him, but at each other. It took Ka Lem a while to realize what they were doing, particularly as his ability to observe or put two thoughts together was seriously lacking.

The priests were connecting themselves together.

Ka Lem blamed the herbs they kept feeding him, but sometimes he could swear he saw golden lines hanging between the priests, glistening like spiderwebs covered in dew.

It wouldn't be a single priest who performed the great magic necessary to take the souls of all the Wind People. No, it would be every priest of the Bone People bound together, working as a single entity.

Would their magic work? Could they take the souls of an entire people? Ka Lem didn't know. Anjr hadn't told him of any failures that the priests had suffered with the elk, if they'd had to kill more than one of them in order to take all their souls.

According to her, all they needed was one.

At least Daleki hadn't survived. Ze had died. The priests had asked Ka Lem if there was anything he knew to help the Stone Person, bringing him to zir body. It had turned into a lifeless pile of stones, never to move again.

When Ka Lem woke from his dream of dancing before the gods, he found himself hanging from a tree, his arms spread wide, his feet not touching the ground. He shook his head, trying to clear his bleary eyes.

All he saw was a dark ocean of priests before him. They wore black robes over their regular clothes, each looking like a piece of the abyss itself. They all bore knives that shone with the light of the golden net that connected them together.

The priests had already begun the ceremony, chanting and praying to their dark god. To that creature Ka Lem had been dancing above in his dream.

Valtyr wasn't a part of this ceremony of theirs, but they didn't know that.

Ka Lem wasn't in a position to tell them, either.

Slowly, the priests started to form a long line, snaking out across the open space in front of Ka Lem. How many were there? A hundred? A thousand? He couldn't say for certain. Just a swelling of black with sharp points of gold wavering in front of him.

The first of the priests stepped up in front of Ka Lem. His gray hair and wrinkles marked him as much older than any of the others. He said a quick prayer, waving his knife in front of Ka Lem's torso, mesmerizing Ka Lem with the light.

The first cut took his breath away. It was shallow, barely a scratch, though it was enough to break the skin and draw a bead of blood down his side.

The priest bowed deeply to Ka Lem, as if thanking him for the honor of cutting him. Then the priest walked away and the next came up. Another short prayer. Another sharp cut.

Ka Lem shuffled his feet, trying to remember the dance. It would save him. He knew that. If he could only remember how.

But the priests kept coming up, their cuts distracting him.

Bright spots of pain broke out all across Ka Lem's torso. He was bleeding from over a dozen shallow cuts now. The time between each cut was shorter. The priests walked faster, sometimes only mumbling a short phrase before striking out with their knives, which seemed to glow much brighter now.

Sweat poured down Ka Lem's body, mingling with the blood so it appeared as though he cried with his entire skin. The words of the priests now tugged at his soul. Darkness nibbled at his feet, as it had in the dream, stopping when he remembered the dance.

The wood against Ka Lem's back felt hard, unyielding. The roots of the tree—a maple, he believed—went deep. This tree had been shading this corner of the marketplace for decades, before the Bone People had set up their market here. It was one of the few trees that had survived the famine. Maybe because the priests had protected it, marking it as sacred.

Though the leaves had all been swept clean from the base of the tree, Ka Lem still saw them. Could feel them as well, hanging about his head, being tickled by the winds.

Leaves started to bloom out of the blood that trickled down his shins. Not the bright green of summer, no, the brooding red of fall. He saw the pattern they formed, the five points.

Ka Lem and the rest of the Wind People could only take the form of animals. None of their myths had even hinted at someone taking the form of a tree or a bush. And it was only the villains in their stories who took on partial forms, like Lan Gi, who could bring up the fur of a wolf while at the same time maintaining her Wind Person form.

And yet…Ka Lem felt the tree reaching for him. Or maybe he was just melding with the tree, pressing against it to get away from the wall of pain inflicted by the priests.

There was something there. Something about the tree. The leaves. The tickling wind.

Ka Lem remembered Gan Ou telling him that she felt as though she needed someone to teach her magic, to fill those holes she'd discovered deep inside herself.

No teacher was going to magically appear before Ka Lem.

Maybe one was already there, though, at his back.

Since he was dying anyway, Ka Lem opened himself up to the tree behind him, begging for her help.

Wind suddenly raced around him. The priests closest to him felt it. It plucked at the golden wires connecting them, twanging them with a sour note, drawing the wires tight.

Several priests came forward all at the same time. Instead of just lightly cutting him, they took their golden knives and stabbed him, sinking the blades deep beneath the skin.

That appeared to be what Ka Lem and the tree needed. He sucked the golden light out of each blade, drawing all that magic into himself, then directing it upward, using the sharp edges of the knives to rip apart the ropes tying him up.

Ka Lem staggered when he found himself standing on his own feet, no longer bound.

The priests paused, confused, possibly scared.

Their hesitation saved Ka Lem. If they had rushed at him immediately, stabbed him again, he wouldn't have been able to fend them off. But they paused, unsure, giving Ka Lem the time to find the winds.

Drawing a deep breath, Ka Lem called the winds to him. All of them. Every dead or dried leaf anywhere in the city flew to him as well, surrounded him like armor, constantly swirling and shifting. The brown of the leaves changed to bright red, like the maple leaves did in the fall. He knew he no longer had the appearance of a Wind Person, but rather, of a pillar of leaves, whirling as if in a cyclone.

The priests in front of Ka Lem did *not* appeared

surprised. Instead, they looked either angry or frightened. Had they known of this ability of the Wind People? Did the Bone People have a myth of Wind People with their leaf armor? Had the two Peoples come into conflict before?

It didn't matter now. Ka Lem used his winds like whips, forcing the priests back, bowling them over in his rage. He found that he had the same power they did to sip at another's life force. He drained all that he touched, healing himself and regaining his wits, his strength, his muscles, even his endurance.

But no more. He recognized the deep dark path that lay before him if he continued. How easy it would be to take more, to make himself more.

That was the trap the being of darkness had laid.

He was too stubborn to go down that way. He only took enough to recover what the Bone People had taken from him. Not a drop more.

Moving like a tornado, Ka Lem blew through the area. He knocked down all the tents, ripping the one he'd been kept in to shreds. He followed the scent of the herbs that had been fed to him to keep him witless, tearing apart both the shop that had sold them as well as the gardens.

He targeted the temples of Valtyr next, knocking down their towers and ramming his way through their sanctuaries, leaving a wide swath of destruction in his path.

Finally, Ka Lem felt the strength of the tree starting to drain away. There was only so much he could do. He could not completely destroy a large city, not on his own, not in a single day.

Not without help.

Ka Lem flung himself at the river, transforming easily into a flock of ducks. Normally, it took many years of training for a Wind Person to maintain form in a collection of creatures. The leaves had taught him the way of it, though.

He knew that the Bone People would be searching for a single large animal. They'd probably shoot at any oversized bird flying through the skies, or even a big wolf. They would have to kill every duck they came across in order to get to Ka Lem, if they could figure out how he'd transformed.

Exhausted, Ka Lem stubbornly flew out of the city, until he found a quiet pond connected to one of the nearby farms. All his disparate parts descended, skimming as they landed on the water. The flock collectively swam to a shallow area at the edge of the pond. Hidden in among the reeds, he tucked his various heads under his wings and allowed himself to be taken away by the first peaceful darkness he'd encountered in a long, long time.

WHEN KA LEM AWOKE, he debated whether or not to head straight back to the Wind People's lands to get reinforcements, or whether to attack the Bone People's capital city again.

There could be no peace between them. He didn't care what the Sea People thought about war. The Bone People wouldn't stop. Not unless Ka Lem and his People killed all the priests. Or at least enough of them so that their magic could no longer work. It was the only way his People, all the Peoples, could be safe.

Could other Wind People find the magic Ka Lem had stumbled into? He felt certain that they could. Hopefully they could do it without having to be driven to the same extreme he had been.

If nothing else, the Wind People would have to find their winds. That much he could help with. He'd chosen to become a teacher, what felt like many lifetimes ago now. He didn't just want to destroy. He wanted to help his People become more than they had been.

With a tired heart, Ka Lem waited until dusk before he took off, the entire flock rising as one. He wouldn't be able to get as far in a group like this as he could as a single large creature. Hopefully, by tomorrow, he'd be far enough away from the capital and all pursuit that he'd be able to change forms into something larger and faster, that would get him home quicker.

Ka Lem wasn't looking forward to the upcoming battles. He was no warrior. He wasn't even a hunter. However, he would do anything to protect his People.

Loudly honking, Ka Lem flew on into the sunset, knowing he'd be crossing these lands again soon enough.

***

KA LEM HAD ACTUALLY BEEN LOOKING FORWARD to blowing down the wall of mist, fog, and smoke that the Bone People had originally used to hide behind. However, he never saw it. He did feel what he thought was a trace of it as he passed over.

That made Ka Lem pause and fly back, circling over the area.

Yes, in the middle of a plain field, he felt a thin golden line of power. It traveled roughly north-south, along the line the wall had once manifested.

Would the magic ever completely fade away? Or would it be held now in the land itself, waiting for those who could sip at it?

Ka Lem would have to land to touch it. He decided to fly on, eager to reach his own People.

He'd been taking the form of a large, black-headed goose,

as it was the quickest of the flying birds, and the one that could fly for the longest without having to take a break.

While Ka Lem wanted to joyously fly into the first village he ran across, the smell of foul smoke on the winds made him cautious.

What mischief had the Bone People been getting into while he'd been gone?

He transformed from a single large goose into a flock of bushtits. Though the birds were small, they frequently traveled in huge flocks, so he hopefully wouldn't be noticed as he flew through the surrounding trees.

What he found horrified him. Bone People maintained fires at the cardinal points of the village. The smoke clung to his wings, coating them with soot, making it difficult to fly.

Most of the Wind People went about their business in the village as if everything were normal. They weren't witless, like he'd been kept. But something was off. Something was very wrong, and it wasn't just the smoke.

It took Ka Lem a third pass around the village before he finally figured out what the problem was: the grass on the village square was overgrown.

No one was dancing.

Ka Lem's ready rage overcame him. He flew out of the trees in the form of a tornado, his winds whipping through the village, clearing the air of the awful smoke. Then he attacked the foul fires, scattering the ashes and tearing apart the Bone People who'd been maintaining them.

He didn't pay attention to any of the other damage such winds might inflict. The Bone People needed to be destroyed, their magic banished.

When he finished, he retook his Wind Person form, standing in the center of the village square. He stood proudly, waiting for his People to come and recognize him.

The fear in the eyes of his own People bothered him. Then again, he had just appeared as a tornado of wind.

An elderly man finally walked forward from the silent group that had gathered. "What did you do?" he asked. The nasal whining tone of his voice bothered Ka Lem.

"I removed the Bone People from your village," Ka Lem said proudly. "The air is now clean. Can't you smell it?"

"Aye," the old man said. He fixed a beady eye on Ka Lem. "And you destroyed the huts that were next to the fires. As well as blew over the trees there."

Ka Lem shrugged. A wind as powerful as his was difficult to control. After a moment, he realized that the elder wanted more of a response. "I freed you." Didn't the Wind People realize they'd been taken over? That their will had been dampened? Why else would they allow the Bone People and their foul magic in their home?

The elder shook his head. "No. We weren't taken, not like the other villages. We still had our will and our wits. All we had to do was to put up with their smoke. You didn't need to kill them all like that."

Ka Lem held himself very still. The awful magic of the Bone People had sunk deeply into the elder.

"When was the last time you danced for Sune Li?" Ka Lem asked in response. "How much have you celebrated?"

The elder looked uneasy for the first time.

Ka Lem gestured around him. "You no longer dance," he said. "How free were you actually?"

Before the elder could say anything, another person came forward. She bore robes that were generally given to travelers coming through an area. "Yes, the destruction was great," she said, shooting a hard look at the other elder. "But so is our thanks." She gave him a smile and waited as Ka Lem slipped the robe over his shoulder. "Maybe you could lead us in a dance of celebration."

"Gladly," Ka Lem said.

A younger person came forward, carrying a drum. She started a lively beat.

Suddenly, people came pouring out of their huts, converging on the square. They formed circles of ten or twelve and started dancing, a soft forward and backwards motion as they held each others' hands tightly.

Ka Lem saw tears streaming down the faces of more than one of the dancers.

They started with a shuffling step that slowly built momentum. Dancers started breaking off from the main circles doing a swirling dance all on their own. They shouted and lifted their arms, dancing feverishly with all their might. Ka Lem thought he saw some of them start their own mini whirlwinds as they rediscovered their power.

A flickering wave appeared to go through the Wind People, starting at the corner and shooting out. With a gladdened cry, first one, then the another of the villagers would suddenly transform into a different shape. It wasn't a long change, just for a moment or two. Then they would come back to their Wind Person form and dance harder.

It was as if they'd forgotten their traditions, forgotten their forms, and were only now rediscovering that they could change into animal shapes.

The elder who'd first greeted Ka Lem passed by, his expression still sour. He moved more slowly in the dance than the others. It was obvious that he still blamed Ka Lem for something.

Yes, they would have to rebuild the parts of their village that Ka Lem had unintentionally destroyed. But more importantly, they'd have to rebuild their hearts and their traditions. He would be sure to suggest to the female elder that the village needed to dance together often, at least at first.

Ka Lem had hoped that he'd just be able to come back home and pick up warriors, heading immediately back to the capital of the Bone People before they had a chance to ready themselves.

Now, his plans were uncertain. Did he need to save as many of his people as he could first before they could go back and destroy all the priests? Stop the threat of the Bone People once and for all?

HY YUN, the drummer from the first village, accompanied Ka Lem to the next town. At the advice of the female elder, they were only going to stop at two of the larger cities on their way north to Shan Yu, the capital. The Wind People could help each other break free, as long as the major towns and villages were taken care of.

Hy Yun's curly brown hair had a tawny tint to it, that in the sunshine appeared to light up her entire face, as her infrequent smile did. She was actually two years older than Ka Lem's twenty years of age, though he felt ancient around her. She stood exactly his same height of five foot, three inches, and while his skin was the color of a dried oak leaf, she was the color of dried birch wood, pale and golden.

Ka Lem was used to either traveling by himself, or with a group. He'd never worked with just one other person before. It felt as though he had a new skill to learn.

Plus, having just one other person around allowed him time to remember how to be a Wind Person, and not just an angry, vengeful wind.

They stopped on the outskirts of their next target. Hy Yun had carried her drum with her, strapped to her body even in an animal form. Now, she took on her Wind Person form, though she stayed up high in the trees, waiting while Ka Lem transformed into a flock of bushtits again.

It was as bad as the first village, though with a much larger area to cover, there were twice as many fires. He flew back to where Hy Yun waited, coalescing into his Wind Person form on the branch beside her.

She rewarded him with a huge smile. "I can't wait to learn how to do that someday," she confessed.

Ka Lem was suddenly happy that his skin was dark enough to hide a blush. He quickly explained what he'd seen.

There was no possible way for him to destroy the fires without doing additional damage. However, hopefully this time he'd have help.

Hy Yun flew into the town first, landing in the center of the main village square. Like the first village, grass overgrew the area. She transformed and started to play her drum, calling the people to her, waking their souls.

Ka Lem transformed into his vengeful tornado form and started destroying the outermost ring of fires, tearing apart every Bone Person he found. He tried to be more careful this time and not blow over all the nearby buildings. He was only partially successful.

By the time Ka Lem got to the last two fires, he found the locals had already started his work for him. He wasn't sure if it was better or not for the townspeople to attack the Bone People. They hadn't lost their transformation abilities, or forgotten them as quickly as the first village. Lumbering bears made quick work of the Bone People who'd been tending the last fires, growling at each other over who got to tear the bodies apart. The Wind People destroyed the fires as well, stomping on the ashes, kicking the coals far apart, even going so far as to break apart the woods stacked nearby.

The town held much more rage than the village had. There were People here who'd only pretended to be cowed, who were as angry at their neighbors as they were at themselves.

Hy Yun called them together with her drum to the large square. Ka Lem helped, blowing the sound of her drum to the far corners of the town. Those who had been fighting were slow to respond, still wanting to rend and tear at the world. Ka Lem herded them as best he could, urging them forward.

It would take a long while for the scars to heal, Ka Lem knew. The dancing would help. Other musicians took up the beat, and soon a lively band had formed, with wooden flutes and clay ocarinas joining in with the many drums.

Ka Lem paused at the edge of the crowd, watching. One of the townspeople noticed him there and approached bearing a traveler's robe. Ka Lem gratefully put it on and stayed where he was, merely shuffling his feet from side to side rather than joining in.

It didn't feel right. The townspeople needed each other, not this stranger in their midst.

And yet…it seemed as if the townspeople all recognized that he was there, watching over them. They passed in front of him, one by one, giving him warm smiles and bowing their heads.

That hadn't been why he'd stayed out of the group of dancers. He didn't want their adoration, though he appreciated their acknowledgement.

What legends would be spoken about him to future generations? What tales would parents and teachers end up telling their children?

It wasn't something he could worry about right now.

As the dancing continued, Ka Lem realized that a part of him wanted to get going, to leave tonight so he and Hy Yun could start their journey to the last large town before they went to Shan Yu. However, he knew they couldn't. He needed to talk with the elders, help them form a plan for how to free the next town over. Teach what winds he could to those who would learn.

He couldn't see Hy Yun playing at the center of the whirling crowd, though he could still distinguish her drum from the others, lively enough to set even a slow bear's feet to moving. So he continued to dance as his People started the slow process of healing themselves.

Chapter Five

STONE

SUGAOSHI SHUDDERED as Noalanon finally shattered the damned iron bar that had been holding zir in place for weeks. The sound of breaking steel echoed loudly in zir ears. Ze tried to sit up immediately, but nearly fell off the table ze had been laying on. Two of zir rescuers came up beside zir, slowly drawing zir up, then supporting zir in a seated position.

There was no shame in being so weak. Or so ze told zirself. Or in feeling as though ze wanted to cry all the damned time.

"Here." One of the specialists in the room shoved another spoonful of minerals at Sugaoshi. They were black with glittering white flecks. Ze obediently opened zir mouth. They had a sweet, honeyed taste, and the crunch was very satisfying.

Ze immediately felt the difference in zir limbs, zir fingers regaining their cleverness. The world grew more solid, as well, as if a barrier had been melted. Slowly, ze pulled away from zir supporters, struggling to regain the ability to sit up on zir own.

Only one of the other former prisoners was in the same room as Sugaoshi. The others had been separated off, each going to a different house to be taken care of. Sugaoshi assumed that the rescuers would be able to identify the witless ones quickly enough. Hopefully, there would now be time to find a cure for their wandering minds.

Sugaoshi took another deep breath, smelling the comforting scents of a home—the scent of warm, baking rocks in the hearth, the faint scent of flowers in the garden in the back, even the lemony smell of the cleaner this family used on their floor.

Slowly, Sugaoshi stretched zir arms out full for the first time in over a month. There was no shame in how zir hands trembled. The specialist fed zir two more bites of the black minerals, along with a spoonful of a brown mineral that coated zir tongue with a warm, spicy flavor.

The group was in a cozy living room. Beautiful black, white, and gray mosaics covered the walls, looking like tall mountains with stylized winds blowing around them. It made her feel safe and secure with such beauty and strength surrounding her. The couches and chairs had been shoved against the wall to make room for the two tables the former prisoners lay on as well as the rest of the rebels, but Sugaoshi could tell that it was all finely made, covered in rich gold and green embroidered material.

A third table held a large array of stone containers for minerals. The two specialists were mixing up different concoctions for their charges. The one attending Sugaoshi approached, this time with a spoonful of minerals that were primarily white with just a tinge of pink. These tasted bitter to zir and were difficult to chew. However, once ze'd swallowed them down, ze felt more strength flooding into zir limbs.

"How are you feeling?" Noalanon asked as the last of the

manacles dropped to the flagstone covered floor with a satisfying clang.

"First, I'd like to soak in a hot bath for a week." Ze took the next spoonful—the brown again—then finally was handed a fine green stone cup filled with a heavenly tea for zir to sip at. "Then I'd like to sleep for a second week. And then start painting, maybe for two full weeks, after that."

Noalanon smiled. "I can offer you a bath, and possibly a nap, but then we need your help."

"I know," Sugaoshi said. She sighed, trying to prepare zirself for the inevitable questions. "One of the others, when they came in, said that you'd had your wits taken from you."

Noalanon nodded. "It took me a while to come back to myself," ze said. "I'm sorry it took so long for us to rescue you."

Sugaoshi waved off Noalanon's apologies. "Bah. Don't worry about it. Sure, it would have been nice to get out of there sooner. But I wouldn't have learned as much as I did if you'd come a week earlier."

Ze looked down at zir side, where the long cuts had finally been washed. Ze couldn't do much about them for now. A salve had been applied, and as soon as it dried, one of the helpers had a long bandage to wrap around zir torso. The pain was more of a memory, a dull ache at the back of zir mind, rather than the sharp prodding fear of how close ze was to death.

"They were trying to figure out how to kill us easily," Sugaoshi said softly. "As it appears that we have a natural ability to resist their magic. Which they didn't know about until their king showed up."

"I'm sorry—" Noalanon started.

"Don't," Sugaoshi said sharply. "Time for regret has long since passed. Don't you think I regret the council's decision to let those damned Bone People stay in the first place? We should have killed them all at that point. Captured them. Something."

Noalanon took a deep breath, swallowing whatever other words ze might have said, nodding instead.

"We will never forget what they have done to us," Sugaoshi promised. Ze was going to have a word with the archivist about how to record all of what happened for future generations, even if it ended up as myths and legends.

But that was for another day.

Ze sighed again, then pushed zir tiredness to the side. There was much work to be done.

"Originally, I had a much smaller group that was going to act as a distraction, on the far side of the temple, while a second group, of builders, attacked the temple itself," Sugaoshi said. Ze reeled off their names. "Then a group of hunters who would take charge of the Bone People." Ze listed off more names.

"But you said that won't work, now," Noalanon said.

"No, not without some changes. Your tunnel will come in handy," Sugaoshi said. "I'd planned on something like that in my modified plans."

Ze started listing zir new plan, which was much better, the attack much more spread out against the stronghold of the Bone People. The attackers would come at the temple from all sides instead of a single, forward push. In addition, Stone People could now pour out of the tunnel they'd already dug. Perhaps a new, smaller tunnel could be added to the side, so they wouldn't all be coming out from the same place.

"The Bone People know that we can resist their prayers," Sugaoshi said. "And they know how we can harden our skin. I refused to do it for them, even when they sliced me with their knives." Ze held up zir hand to postpone yet another apology from Noalanon. "They will be prepared with obsidian knives. The hunters who go against the Bone People must be prepared to be injured. Possibly killed."

Noalanon's eyes grew wide, but then ze nodded.

Sugaoshi grimaced. Yes, as ze had expected. The raid had gone well. No one had been killed.

However, the Stone People were going to have to face the fact that they would have to kill those who had tried to oppress them, if they wanted to be free.

And that would be the most difficult thing of all.

⁂

"IT HAS TO BE ME," Sugaoshi patiently said again. "I need to be the distraction." Ze sat with the other leaders, half a dozen, all crowded around a small eating table. The minerals the specialists had served zir had done wonders for how good ze felt. Ze understood, though, that ze would need some time to build zirself up to full strength.

For today, what ze had would have to be enough.

Ze'd spent at least an hour in a heated tub the night before, soaking away the aches and scum inflicted on zir by the Bone People. Someone sat with zir the entire time, making sure that ze didn't pass out and drown accidently.

Then ze got to sleep in a bed. A real bed! With sheets and blankets and warmth and comfort.

Sugaoshi didn't sleep as well as ze had expected. Ze kept waking up, thinking that reality was a dream, that ze hadn't escaped.

"I don't want to have to come and rescue you again," Hirshamin growled. Ze had been a traveler with Noalanon, and now was nominally in charge of the renegade builders.

"You won't if you do your job," Sugaoshi snapped at Hirshamin. "But I have to act as the distraction. The priests won't know what to do about me. Particularly if I claim, at first, that they've cured me."

"How did you resist their prayers?" Noalanon asked.

Sugaoshi smiled. Ze could tell that Noalanon had been wanting to ask that question for a long while.

"You said that it was your partner who brought you back, yes?" Sugaoshi asked.

Noalanon nodded.

"And you said it was your children?" Sugaoshi said, turning to Hirshamin.

"Aye, it was," the builder said. Zir smile was soft with the memory of it.

"It's always a connection with something outside of yourself," Sugaoshi said. "That's what seemed to work on the other prisoners. They might wander lost for a while, but reminding them of their connections would bring them back."

Ze paused, remembering the urgent whispers the prisoners had exchanged, chained up and unable to protect themselves. "For me, it was my art. Those assholes were trying to strip that from me." Ze had many rude words to say about that, rants that ze had gone through more than once in zir head. "My connection to my art is what allowed me to keep my wits, in the end."

Sugaoshi knew that Noalanon wanted to ask more questions. Now wasn't the time.

"So whatever it is that the idiotic priests throw at me, it won't work," Sugaoshi said. "I will stay me. They cannot take my wits away. Therefore, it must be me who acts as the distraction. The priests won't know what to do about it."

"What's to stop them from just filling you with arrows?" one of the hunters asked. "Or dropping weighted nets on you?"

"They'd have to declare that I'm an enemy, not someone

who could possibly be saved," Sugaoshi said. "And they wouldn't attack me in front of a crowd. Their plans are not yet all in place." Ze grimaced. "They will also want to know how we escaped. Trust me. I am the largest distraction you could have."

Sugaoshi knew that ze was right. This arguing was yet another way to delay the inevitable attack. Zir people didn't move quickly. They also weren't killers.

There was no other way.

"We will do it your way," Hirshamin finally said, nodding. Ze paused, growing still for a moment. "And we need to go now."

Finally! Sugaoshi tried to conceal zir impatience as they all got up from the table, slowly making their way to the door.

The air held the chill from the evening, clear and crisp. Sugaoshi found zirself taking deep breaths, as if cleansing zir lungs still. Once this was over, ze might camp out in the backyard of zir house, staying outside for days at a time and never being trapped inside again.

When they reached the cross street, Sugaoshi froze.

There was the holy mountain.

Ze drank in the majestic sight of it. While the specialists' minerals had done wonders, sight of the holy mountain filled zir with a different kind of strength: the endurance of eternity, to not let anything so petty as a few bones knock zir down. The white, snow-capped peak purified zir heart, the way the clouds wreathed the top made zir straighten up and stand taller, and the incredible blue of the sky made zir want to fill the entire world with songs of praise.

It would take zir the rest of zir life to capture the feeling ze had upon viewing the mountain again after so long.

That, however, was yet another thing for later.

Sugaoshi made zir feet move forward again, though both

Hirshamin and Noalanon nodded at zir. They'd recently traveled, and remembered their first sight of the mountain as well.

The group split up, with Noalanon going to the icehouse with those planning on breaching the temple from the inside, Hirshamin heading toward the back of the temple with the other builders, and the hunters dispersing widely.

Sugaoshi took a deep breath as they neared the busy marketplace. While there were many people already up and about, the market wasn't as crowded as it once had been. Ze told zirself that it was all right—the Stone People could rebuild their connections, find their joy again.

Though Sugaoshi wore a large dark-brown cloak as ze walked toward the temple, and ze kept zir head down, people appeared to recognize zir anyway.

Some gasped and hurried away. Ze didn't blame them for being scared, for understanding at a fundamental level that a fight was on the way.

More, however, followed in zir wake as ze approached the temple.

Sugaoshi had never felt uncertain near mere stone before. Fear still struck zir, deep in zir core. A part of zir wanted to cry out that it was too soon for zir to confront zir captors. Ze wasn't ready yet. Zir heart was still battered and sore, and zir body hadn't fully healed.

Ze had no choice. Better to throw down this false god and its People than suffer another day. Sugaoshi made zirself be still, despite how zir knees wanted to wobble and zir hands tremble. Zir stomach knotted, and the ache of hunger still lingered despite the wonderful minerals ze had been fed.

The walls of the temple lifted far above Sugaoshi's head. Ze didn't stand too close to them—ze didn't want the Bone People to just be able to drop a net on zir head.

The walls were such a pretty rose-gold color. Finely made,

of course, the blocks fitting tightly together, making the walls seem seamless. Zir People would do nothing less than that, even when it came to a foreign temple.

However, those stones were sucking out the life of zir People. They were tainted with zir People's blood. They could be reused, made into a different monument, at some point.

Nothing was ever wasted. Or at least that was what Mana used to say.

Sugaoshi paused for another moment, taking a deep breath, wishing that perhaps instead of just painting, ze could have focused on a different art, such as acting.

It had to be now.

Using a large, dramatic movement, Sugaoshi threw off the cloak that ze had been wearing. Though ze had hated putting back on the dirty, stained, and cut up jacket that ze had worn while in captivity, ze couldn't think of a better visual testamony to a crowd to show how badly ze had been treated.

"People of Killapany! Hear me! It is I, Sugaoshi, returned to you!"

Sugaoshi used every trick ze had ever heard about to make zir words loud enough for a crowd to hear. It appeared to be working, as all the noise at this end of the marketplace suddenly died down. "I bring you news! Great news!" ze called out.

People seemed interested in what ze had to say, and started gathering around zir.

"You need to heed me! Heed the great magic of the Bone People!" Sugaoshi continued.

That struck a chord of unease with the slowly gathering crowd. Ze heard the grumbling but continued on with the plan.

"You can see how they treated me!" Sugaoshi said. "I am well, now. Cleaned of any bad influences!"

People were uncertain what Sugaoshi meant. A crowd of Bone People guards suddenly pushed their way forward.

"See? Your saviors!" Sugaoshi called out.

That made the guards pause. Obviously they'd been told to apprehend Sugaoshi, assuming that ze would accuse them of, well, the truth of what had happened to zir.

"They have come to share word of their god with us!" Sugaoshi said. "The great Valtyr!"

A wave of unease went through the crowd again, delighting Sugaoshi. Ze beamed at zir audience.

Maybe ze should consider a second career in acting.

What the guards couldn't see was how the Stone People looked up, glancing above the temple at the holy mountain before refocusing back on Sugaoshi.

Finally, Sugaoshi saw that the hunters ze'd met the night before were standing in place, surrounding the guards.

"But we all know that the great Valtyr cannot overcome Kiproary," Sugaoshi said. "We cannot live in the abyss. We need the firmament under our feet. The guiding light of Sune Li. The wisdom of ages passed down with Ishkra. And the holy mountain which shines above us."

People in the crowd nodded, easier with this turn in Sugaoshi's speech. While of course, Kiproary was the most important of all the gods, singling out just one god wasn't right. All the gods had their place. Even Valtyr, the god of the darkness.

The guards, on the other hand, weren't pleased. They started to push themselves forward again, only to find themselves suddenly hemmed in on all sides by hunters.

"You will not take me captive again," Sugaoshi warned. Ze spread zir arms wide. "You can see how well I was cared for," ze said. Ze held up the side of zir jacket that had been cut. "See how kindly the priests dealt with my flesh."

A gasp ran through the crowd as they spied the unhealed

wounds. It had hurt so much to take off the bandages. But Sugaoshi would not be deterred.

"They held me, bound me with iron, so that I could never escape," Sugaoshi said. One of the hunters threw the iron bar that had been Sugaoshi's constant companion for all those weeks. It landed with an ominous thunk at zir feet. Ze wrapped zir fingers around the chill metal. For a moment ze almost faltered, the memory of being imprisoned overwhelming zir.

No. They did not get to win.

Slowly, ze lifted the bar up above zir head. "This is how they would bind us all! With iron and chains!"

The crowd gave an angry murmur.

A priest poked up above the wall. "Would you believe a mad female?" he called out.

Sugaoshi nearly laughed at the priest's mistake. "A female?" ze challenged. "I am no female! I am a person! A Stone Person!"

Before the priest could challenge again, Sugaoshi continued.

"You hear what they think of us? How they mistreat us? We do not need to stand for it. You do not need this yoke around your neck." Ze shook the iron bar above zir head. "Would you bind your children this way?"

Dark clouds drifted over the temple walls. There must be a dozen or more priests in the temple tower.

Good.

"Hold each other's hands!" Sugaoshi called out. "Feel the strength and connection of your neighbors. Raise your internal temperature! Do not allow the foreigner's filth to control you!"

The hunters in the crowd who weren't surrounding the guards did as Sugaoshi asked, holding out their hands and getting the others to grab on.

It was those connections that would save them. Sugaoshi had no doubt of that.

The crowd growled loudly as their anger was shared and multiplied.

"Tear down the walls of your prison!" Sugaoshi commanded. "Tear down the blight that has taken hold of our fair city! Remember your bedrock! Hold onto your family, your friends, your heritage!"

Two of the builders that Sugaoshi had recruited earlier hurried forward. They placed their hands on the wall just behind Sugaoshi and *pushed* with their magic and their might.

The creaking of stone rose above the angry shouts of the crowd.

Arrows rained down from the temple walls.

The screams of injured Stone People shredded pieces from Sugaoshi's soul.

"Harden your skin! Don't let them get to you!" she urged.

It wouldn't be enough. Sugaoshi had known that from the beginning.

People, innocent people, were going to die today.

But those priests would also die today.

The crowd that Sugaoshi had gathered seemed to evenly divide itself. Half ran away, back to their homes, away from the conflict and danger, while the rest ran forward. A line of Stone People formed, all pushing against the walls that they, themselves, had built. Sugaoshi watched muscles straining and feet slipping as the people pushed into the stone. Ze continued to exhort zir People, encouraging them to keep going, to push with all their might.

Cracks appeared along the rose-gold rocks. Imperfections formed where once had been just smoothness. Dust filled the air, carrying with it the smell of freshly milled stone.

They were doing it! The Stone People were going to succeed!

Blackness poured over the top of the walls, trying to restrain the crowd. The remembered filth made Sugaoshi gag.

A few desperate guards threw their nets down, trying to stop those pushing. Sugaoshi dragged the closest nets off the backs of the workers, gasping as ze felt the strength leave zir hands. Others in the crowd saw zir actions and followed suit.

A loud rumble shook the ground. Sugaoshi feared for a moment that perhaps one of the Stone People had gone too far in their anger, reaching deep into the earth to draw up the boulders hidden there in order to fling them, like the villain Jakolani had.

The shouting jubilation that floated in the air told Sugaoshi what had happened. The rear wall of the temple had just collapsed. The group of builders who had first attacked had demolished their portion of it.

"Push!" Sugaoshi demanded. "Your lives, your children's lives, depend on it! Push!"

The grinding of stones as the wall fell inward was music to zir ears. How could ze capture the trembling of the earth in a painting? The glory of the clear view of the holy mountain shining down on them? The anger and fear of the crowd as Bone People guards and priests came pouring out of the buildings inside the complex? The sour smell of fear mingled with the freshness of the earth?

A kaleidoscope of images washed before Sugaoshi. The hunters who'd hung back springing to the fore, brandishing javelins and knives. Two of those who'd pushed down the wall stopping to shift one of the large square stones that had fallen backwards and was crushing the leg of one of their companions. The nets glistening with magic as the Bone People guards flung them high above their heads, how they sailed through the air. The angry roar of Stone People finally goaded into action.

Sugaoshi found zirself confronting one of the priests, the one who'd seemed to take the most pleasure in taunting zir.

"We should have killed you as soon as we took you in," the priest declared as he sliced at Sugaoshi with a black, obsidian blade.

Sugaoshi put an arm up to defend zirself. The cut was bright and sharp, making zir screech with anger as much as pain.

"You missed your chance," Sugaoshi taunted as ze grabbed the arm of the priest, before he could strike at zir again.

"You're an abomination. All of you," the priest said after he tried hitting Sugaoshi with his other hand to no effect. All he ended up doing was bruising his flesh on zir hardened skin.

"So are you," Sugaoshi said, reaching for his neck.

Sugaoshi didn't know how to kill a person. Not intentionally. Ze still caught the priest's throat in zir hand and started to squeeze slowly, inexorably, zir hand as implacable as any stone.

The priest gasped as he lost air. He flailed, striking Sugaoshi's arm with his free hand, trying desperately to get away as ze stole his life. His face turned purple, his eyes bulged out of his head, his tongue suddenly hung out.

Sugaoshi would have stopped at that point. Ze judged the priest to be injured enough that he wouldn't cause any more grief. Plus, ze was quickly losing what strength ze had. The rush of the confrontation was passing, leaving zir panting. Ze had no reserves.

Then the hunter beside zir called out a warning. More guards came rushing forward.

Sugaoshi found the strength in zirself to lift the priest off the ground with the hand crushing his throat. Ze turned and flung the idiot at those who approached, bowling them over.

It wouldn't be enough to stop them.

They all had knives, and ze had nothing left. Ze was an artist, not a fighter. Ze certainly didn't know how to fend off two attackers at once, let along three.

Pain blossomed in Sugaoshi's chest as the first guard rushed forward and struck zir with a knife. Ze tried to catch hold of the hand holding it, but a second knife bit into zir side. Agony stole zir breath, just as ze had stolen air from the priest.

Another sharp pain slid across Sugaoshi's stomach. Ze stumbled to the side, gasping.

No! Ze had so much more to paint. So much art to create.

However, ze had always known that ze would die young, that ze would be called back to Ishkra before zir time.

It was up to the others, now.

Sugaoshi turned and grabbed at the nearest Bone Person. Ze clumsily swung zir arms around. Zir entire body jolted with pain when zir fist connected with the guard's face.

Then Sugaoshi was falling. The blackness rising to greet zir was soft and full of the sound of water.

And that was all ze knew.

Chapter Six

———————————

SEA

AJOOLESS FLOATED in the underground river that connected the wells in the Bone People's capital to the aquifer. Everything was dark and black, but this wasn't the fearful abyss of Valtyr, no, these were the waters of rebirth. The waters healed her, soothing not only her land-ravaged skin but her soul. She floated for a timeless while, soaking up the dreams of the water.

When Ajooless surfaced, she found herself in a body of water that moved more swiftly. It took her a while to separate herself from the healing liquid that carried her, to redefine her water form. She wasn't quite sure what she'd become as she'd dreamed—possibly just free-flowing water itself. That would be the only way she could have passed through the porous rocks of the aquifer. Because now, she was in a river. It was the same river she'd crossed many days ago. The one that was fed by the stream that had such awareness.

It didn't occur to her until much, much later that she might have literally been reborn during her time in the water, becoming the being the water needed.

This river had, at one point, been the far, eastern border

between the River People and the Bone People, who'd originated in the mountains to the east of here. Ajooless had never known of two people who could mate with each other, but the River People and the Bone People had always had that ability. Their powers grew mixed as they intermarried. It was why the Bone People could raise the wall of fog—that had originally been a power of the River People. It was also why the River People now used metal in their boats, which had previously all been made out of wood.

Though it wasn't proper food, Ajooless could still snack on the reeds that grew along the riverbank, as well as the fish, as she regained her strength over the following week. She followed the boats up and down the river, getting a feel for the River People. They still secretly worshipped the old god of the rivers, plaiting river reeds into intricate shapes then dropping the pieces into the water to ask for the god's blessing.

Ajooless felt a kinship with them. Though they didn't have a water form, not like the Sea People, their magic and their lives were still water based. They hated the dry plains, sticking to towns and villages along the rivers and streams instead. It was only the Bone People who'd insisted on farming out in the middle of nowhere, with a well being the only water.

When two boats passed, they would frequently call out to each other, sharing whatever news they had. It pleased her to hear that the capital city had been attacked by a tornado, and all the temples had been destroyed.

Ajooless knew that had been the work of Ka Lem, who'd found his strength before the priests had killed him. Good. It meant that the Wind People could fight back, now.

But what of her people? Back in the city of Shiboleth? She knew that they wouldn't be fully taken by the Bone

People. All they had to do was to stick their hands in water to regain themselves.

They still needed to know her news, and of her plan to sterilize those who carried too much of the blood of the Bone People. It would take many years for the plan to come to full fruition. She felt the need to let Liseth know *now*, to get the wheels moving.

Plus, there was no guarantee that Ajooless would survive crossing the plains again. It would take so many months for her to do it on her own, stopping frequently to find water and heal her land form as she walked.

The best way for Ajooless to carry her news back to Liseth would be for her to speak through a fish again. However, she didn't have the power to do that on her own. She'd need to tap the strength of a group.

As the first week after her escape had passed, Ajooless felt herself recover. She knew she had to leave the waters soon. The big rivers mainly traveled north and south. She started plotting her way back west, following tributaries and smaller streams as often as she could, seeking the way back that would allow her to spend most of her time in the water and not on land.

She fretted about her news, though.

That was when luck struck.

Or fate.

Ajooless knew that future generations would be the ones who would pass final judgement on what occurred.

A larger boat sailed by while Ajooless was contemplating her next steps. Instead of the smaller family boats that comfortably held three to four people, this one was similar to the bigger merchant ships, large enough to carry a crew of two dozen or more. The sail was white, instead of the colorful sails of the River People. In addition, black and white banners hung along the edges of the boat.

Curious, Ajooless swam along behind the boat, trying to determine its purpose. She realized at some level that she was procrastinating. She justified it by telling herself it was important for her to learn everything she could about the Bone People.

It turned out that a large contingent of priests were on the boat. Was it a celebration? The boat made stops now and again, and the priests would stand in a group on the front stoop and pray.

Was this one of the ways the Bone People had originally conquered the River People? By taking a boat and spreading their dark abyss up and down the river? It had that feel, of a ritual that was no longer needed.

It gave Ajooless an idea.

The priests could work together as one. She'd dreamed it, and she'd also seen them do it as they'd prepared for a ritual back in the capital city. She wasn't sure what the purpose was. However, it was obvious to her that they had the same power that she'd been able to tap into, to bind themselves together so that the one leading them could use their collective strength.

That evening, they prayed together, deep in the bowels of the boat. They became a single entity in some sense, performing magic for some purpose she didn't understand.

Though Ajooless didn't know for certain, she'd guess that the power for people to join up came originally from the River People. Drops became trickles, which became streams, which would eventually lead to a torrential river. The individual drop fed into the larger body.

The next time the priests gathered, Ajooless was going to try to reach them, take hold of their power and use it for herself.

She had no idea if it would work. If it would send them

looking for her instead. If they would even notice her attempt.

She still had to try.

AS THE DUSK GATHERED, Ajooless watched the river boats pull over to the banks and cast huge metal anchors to moor them. She suspected that the majority of the River People didn't actually need the anchors—they could use magic to make the boats stand still for an evening. The anchors were merely for show, insisted upon by the Bone People.

The night sky was clear, no clouds to hide the stars. Ajooless felt as though the goddess herself was watching her.

Ajooless floated near the surface of the river, holding onto to the large boat carrying all the priests. The wood had been cleverly shaped, probably by the River People magic. The bow felt smooth under her fingers. It reminded her in some ways of the work she'd seen the Wind People do with wood, smoothing out the edges so a wooden piece of furniture appeared to be whole, and not made out of pieces.

The previous night, the priests had gathered in the bow of the boat, below the surface of the water. It was how she'd felt their magic, the tendrils of the net they drew over themselves, connecting one to the next.

There was no way of knowing if Liseth would be watching the goldfish that Ajooless had used before. Even if Liseth weren't there herself, hopefully the priestess would have set someone to always be at the pond where the goldfish lived, in case Ajooless did reach out to her through it again.

If, that was, Ajooless could do it.

As the night grew blacker above the water, Ajooless felt the priests gather together. Their chanted prayers vibrated through the wood under her palms. She closed her eyes and reached for the golden net they formed, trying to draw the edges of it to her. The strings were as slippery as eels sliding through her fingers. The smell of wet grass wafted toward her, as if the Bone People were remembering being on the open plains above.

If only she could be there on the boat with them! If she could touch them, she might be able to harness their power.

Ajooless shifted her hands wider across the bow of the boat. A nail was lodged in the wood. Not on the external surface of the boat, but on the inside.

It acted as a conduit for the Bone People's magic. They were, after all, iron workers.

Ajooless quickly shifted her other hand, seeking more metal. There it was. She ended up with her hands placed one above the other. Something had been nailed to the wall on the inside of the boat. Maybe a shelf, or possibly a seat.

It didn't matter. The metal was the key. She couldn't draw the tendrils of the magic net with her bare hands. It came easily, though, to the metal nails. All she had to do was to draw the magic through, out to the surface of the boat, then into her own body.

The feeling was both similar and different than when she'd worked with the Sea People. Similar, in that the surge of power thrilled her. It tasted different, however. Instead of being like cool blue lines of wintergreen, the net was hot, like streaks of red pepper drawn along a current. It felt warm as well, her body starting to heat up the cold water around her. If she could have shifted and moved to another location, she would have. Her sea form didn't have a way to sweat, not like her land form. She found herself panting, even though air didn't move in and out of her lungs that way.

Ajooless realized that she didn't have a lot of time. The priests were held together tightly by the net. She used some of her own power to keep them that way, holding them rigid while she drew more magic from them.

Then Ajooless flung her senses out, tracing the waters west to the sea, skipping across the vast expanse of land, seeking the portal she'd established before.

It felt to Ajooless as though she rode a boat in choppy water. Wind blew chilling drops across her body. The porthole she sought rose and lowered with the waves. She smelled the salt of the sea, her entire body shuddering with longing to be back there.

She forced herself forward. There was a way through. She just had to find it.

The world bobbed as she steadied herself. She imagined her thoughts as a golden javelin, lit with the fire from the priests. She heaved it forward, spearing the black dot of the way out.

Suddenly, Ajooless was raising her head above the water. She nearly cried when she recognized the garden of the main temple back home. It was spring and the flowers were madly blooming. Little white flowers with heart-shaped leaves, along with sweet clover, decorated all the spaces between the taller trees. The smell of the ocean came back much more strongly, and she heard the wind whispering her name.

In front of the fountain that Ajooless swam in, she saw an older person seated on a wooden bench. It took her a moment to recognize Sasuelana, Liseth's old acolyte.

For a moment, Ajooless felt the hot rage of jealousy. *She* was supposed to become the head acolyte. What was Sasuelana doing there?

Then it occurred to her that Liseth had, indeed, set a watch on the fountain, for the times when Liseth couldn't be there. The high priestess wouldn't ask just anyone to do this important duty. No, she'd asked the person she felt she could trust the most.

Ajooless made a splashing sound in the fountain, drawing the old person's eyes to her.

Sasuelana wasn't dressed like an acolyte. No, she wore a plain dress. Though the color was a pretty sage green, the dress itself had been repaired more than once, and the cloth was starting to thin with use. Didn't Sasuelana's family have the money to buy her something better? Though the color set off Sasuelana's beautiful blue-tinted skin well, it still gave the impression that she was dowdy.

"Yes?" Sasuelana said. She gasped when she saw the fish with its head poked up above the surface of the water. "You're here!" she exclaimed. "Thank you for the warning. The city is safe because of you."

The warmth that Ajooless felt tripled. Liseth had understood her cryptic comment about bringing the Bone People to her sister's temple. Good.

"I have much to tell you," Ajooless said. "I am still in the lands of the Bone People."

Abruptly, Ajooless felt the world around her grow darker. It was as if the circle she'd shot through had suddenly decreased in size.

What had caused that? Ajooless couldn't take the time to figure it out now. But it did warn her that she didn't have much time.

As quickly as she could, Ajooless explained what had happened, what she had learned. How the Sea People could stop the Bone People over time. How it wouldn't have to end with a war that would bring about the end of the third age.

There was one last thing that Ajooless wanted to try. The porthole was closing fast. Was she draining the power of the priests that quickly? They didn't have the strength of her own People for this type of work, that was for certain.

"Come closer," Ajooless told Sasuelana as she finished.

Ajooless dipped the head of the fish below the surface of

the fountain and caused it to draw in a mouthful of water. Ajooless filled her own mouth with river water. Then she caused the fish to spit the water out, soaking the other woman's chest with the thin stream.

Sasuelana gasped as the waters struck her.

"Those are the waters I'm in!" Ajooless said as the porthole around her closed. "Find them and you'll find the home of the Bone People!"

She wasn't certain if those last words made it to Sasuelana or not. Ajooless found herself sucked through the porthole backwards, flying through the air then under the sea, like a harpoon being drawn back by an impatient hunter.

Suddenly, Ajooless slammed back into her body. She gasped, lifting her hands from the boat she'd been resting her palms against. Her skin tingled and felt bruised, as though she'd fallen on a rocky shore. All of her body ached.

Everything around her was inky black, as though marked by a squid. The water was cold, much colder than it had been. It wasn't healthy, either. There was barely anything for her to breathe left in it. It tasted of mulch and rotten reeds.

Something made her reach out and touch the boat again before she swam away. It, too, seemed dead. She reached for the priests she'd held together earlier, only to find nothing there.

There was no life left on the boat. Not only had Ajooless taken the magic and power of the priests, she'd stolen their lives as well.

Ajooless forced herself up, out of the water. Her lungs filled with air, a sharp pain drilling through her core at the abrupt change.

No one walked on the deck of the boat. All Ajooless saw were dark lumps of bodies.

She'd not only taken the lives of the priests, but of

everyone on board. The boat itself seemed darker as well, as if the wood had been scorched by an inner fire.

How had she done that? She hadn't meant to. She hadn't meant to harm anyone.

As she swam quickly away, she wondered what would be made of her tale. Would she become a great heroine to her people? Or would she be judged a villain?

* * *

AJOOLESS NEEDED another day to recover, floating in the river waters. She found herself drawn to the one small tributary that had such awareness. Though the waters supposedly joined together, there was very little exchange of drops between the two entities. The stream kept to itself, not wanting to dilute its presence by flowing into the main body of water.

What would happen if she went and swam in those waters? What dreams would the water teach her? Would they heal her soul, which ached from the deaths she'd caused? Or would they multiply her shame at having needlessly taken so many lives?

At first, Ajooless merely stuck an arm into the small tributary. The water felt distinctly cooler, as if it was fed from a different underground stream than the river. It took a while for the dreams to sneak up on her as she floated, one hand wrapped firmly around a rock on the riverbed in the stream, anchoring her, while the rest of her stayed out of reach.

This time, however, the stream didn't show her the past, but her future.

Ajooless had grown darker. She knew that was true, but had blamed that on the treatment she'd received when she'd been a prisoner, that she hadn't fully recovered yet.

No, the waters told her. She would stay dark, and grow darker still.

It also showed her that she would not go home. Instead, she would stay in the lands of the Bone People, wreaking havoc every time she ran across a group of priests bound together.

Ajooless cried out at the deaths that accumulated in her path. The coldness of the water surrounding her stole her breath away. She reeked of dead fish and broken dreams.

Was this truly her future? To cause so much suffering? To never swim in the beautiful waters of her homeland again, to never see Shiboleth? Or Sillboden?

Or was this merely what the waters wanted her to become? They were still faithful to the River People and resentful of the Bone People. Did the waters see her as a savior for its People?

Ajooless wrenched her arm out of the stream and flowed up the main river, heading directly to a small, uninhabited area where the waters eddied, where she'd slept a few times previously.

She didn't have to become a killer of the Bone People. All that the Sea People had to do was to sterilize those with too much of the Bone People's blood. It would also kill off those poor wretches in the villages and towns to the east of here, in the mountains. Shut down the mines and poorer towns.

Would it be enough? Eventually, yes, it would be.

In the meanwhile, the Bone People and those damned priests might try again, capturing another one of the Sea People and then trying to steal their souls.

Ajooless couldn't let that happen.

She spent the rest of the long afternoon praying to the goddess, asking for her wisdom, though her prayers were never answered.

NIGHT CAME, and Ajooless still felt unsettled about her future. Maybe if she left the river, spent some time in her land form, she'd feel more determined to make it back to her home.

The thought of changing filled her with dread, making her stomach churn. The waters surrounding her clung to her skin, like a wet blanket, as if the river itself wanted her to remain there.

Slowly, Ajooless climbed out of the water. The bank was full of cold mud that quickly covered her hands and arms when she slipped and fell, making her long to slide back into the water and be clean again. Her lungs creaked every time she tried to take a deep breath, as if they were out of practice gathering oxygen.

Ajooless couldn't see her body clearly—the night was too dim—but she could tell that her hands maintained a little of their webbing between the fingers, and her feet were still too long. They slapped against the ground, quickly growing sore and bruised. Her arms had skin, though when she looked closely, there appeared to still be an impression of scales running in rows across them. Her legs trembled, unused to carrying the weight of her body.

Ajooless had never heard of someone staying too long in their water form, being unable to change fully back to their land form. Was it because she'd been floating in fresh water and not in sea water? Or had her time under the earth changed her? She'd been teased as a child that she looked more like a fish and less like a Sea Person. She wondered if that was truer now.

Still, Ajooless made herself stay out of the water, not allowing herself to merely turn and dive back into the soothing currents of the river, cleansing her body and soul.

She wondered later if that was a mistake.

The sweet smell of fish being cooked over a fire drew her forward. She felt as though she could float on the scent—undulate through the air like an eel through the water toward it. Her mouth watered and her stomach lurched, reminding her of just how empty it felt.

She was so involved following the scent that she nearly stumbled straight into a camp of the Bone People. They had carts, like those she'd traveled on for so long. As well as elk.

Anger seared through Ajooless. Was this another hunting team? Gone to try their luck, fetching one of the Sea People? Or maybe, since Ka Lem had escaped, another of the Wind People?

No. She would not allow that to happen.

There were two priests with this group. They'd bonded together to gather a dark cloud to themselves, to use it to spread a warning about what had happened at the river.

The fire held no food, no crispy fish flesh for her to nibble on.

The smell she'd been following had been the scent of their magic.

Ajooless decided to add her own warning.

She waited until the priests had finished their business, sending a long, complicated message to several of the priests waiting back at the main city. The priests had used the power of all of those surrounding them, the guards as well as the women who cared for the camp. The priests had even connected to the elk standing at the edge of their camp, drawing on their dark fires and power.

Before the priests could disassemble their net, Ajooless grabbed hold of it. It was more difficult in her land form, when she stood in the air and wasn't surrounded by the magic in the waters.

However, the elk had an iron chain drawn over their

necks to keep them still. Ajooless touched the metal with her own power, linking herself to the priests and the thin net they'd set up over the entire campsite.

Then Ajooless *pulled*. She could think of nothing else to describe it. It felt as though she stood on shore and was dragging a large, water-logged net out of the sea. She could smell the salt on the air. Or maybe that was just the sweat of the men. Her mouth filled with ashes, as though she swallowed dirt. The muscles across her shoulders ached as she pulled harder. She felt herself sliding, her feet barely keeping their grip on the land. The backs of her legs stiffened as she forced herself to remain in place.

Ajooless kept pulling, gathering all the threads of magic to herself.

Then she sucked them dry, every last one of them.

She was more conscious of her efforts this time. The first time, she'd done it by accident. This time, she was more aware of the satisfying taste of the magic, sweet and delicate like the finest baked fish. It glided down her throat like golden honey. Her finger swelled with the power, as did her entire body. She grew bloated, as if she'd swallowed down an entire sea.

Once she started, she couldn't have stopped herself if she tried.

She didn't try.

She pulled all the magic and life from the priests, the elk, all the people in the camp, into herself.

When nothing but bitter dregs remained, Ajooless spread her arms wide, lifting her face to the clear sky, then she spewed all that she'd taken out, becoming a living fountain splashing power onto the desiccated earth.

The Bone People had taken from the earth, taken and then taken more, their greed draining everything around them. Ajooless directed the magic that she'd drawn into herself back out into the world.

The dry plains she'd crossed had once had a plethora of rivers, streams, and small lakes running across them. By returning the magic to the land, the water could gather again and the dry plains would heal themselves.

When Ajooless was finished, nothing remained standing at the campsite. Not the tents, not the priests, not the guards—even the elk were now just piles of bones. She'd even stolen the light from the campfire, the ashes grown cold.

Ajooless tried to tell herself that she wouldn't do this again. She made herself walk among the dead, staring into their poor, desiccated faces, trying to make herself feel sorry for what she had done.

In her heart of hearts, all Ajooless felt was the greatest satisfaction, as if she'd just had the finest meal.

She was keeping the Sea People safe. All the Peoples safe. It wasn't just about feeding her own growing need for power and more power, her own selfish needs. She'd spewed out all the power she'd sucked in.

Really.

Chapter Seven

WIND

GAN OU KEPT her winds wrapped around her all the time, even at night, when she tried to sleep. At first, the sound of the constant rushing was soothing to her. It reminded her of the fountains in Killapany, that the Stone People had built for the Sea People to wash their feet in.

Sometimes she grew tired of the whispering winds, longing for peace and quiet.

There would never be peace and quiet for her, though.

Day by day, the Wind People pushed the army of Bone People back to the east, out of their land. Gan Ou kept expecting the Bone People to try to reach a settlement, send ambassadors to negotiate, now that they were losing. They seemed more determined than ever, though, to drive forward and attack.

Gan Ou was now recognized as a teacher of sorts. However, she wasn't good enough to be an elder. She'd never overcome the stigma of being banished. That was fine with her. She had her own cohort of students who would listen to her.

The real break came after the Bone People had been

driven east of Shan Yu. The fighting had been terrible that day. Gan Ou feared that the Wind People were emptying their villages, losing so many to the battles.

All she could do was push forward. Healing the Wind People once the war was finally over would be the job of the elders. She'd be able to retire and would no longer teach children how to call winds that killed.

The night was full of dark clouds and lightning, but no rain, setting Gan Ou's teeth on edge. The weather seemed unnatural, and the smell of death danced all around them. Though Gan Ou's constant winds kept her warm, she still found herself shivering in the middle of the night, a lead weight in her belly.

The next morning, the Bone People's troops seemed diminished. Even in the bright sunlight, they no longer shone pale and golden, but looked wan and drained instead.

What had happened to the morale of their group? There were just as many fighters, just as many priests. They merely seemed determined, though, and not eager to attack.

Had their king been killed? That was what Gan Ou guessed. Someone had finally knifed that bastard.

The fighting was still awful, still desperate. However, the line of the Bone People broke early. Many, too many, were killed when they turned their backs and ran. Even Gan Ou was sickened by how gleefully her people raced after those fleeing.

Late that night, Gan Ou was woken by Pan Su.

"What is it?" she asked, her winds at the ready, spinning small dust devils along her sides.

"The Bone People have called up one of their walls," Pan Su said. "They're now hiding behind it."

"What?" Gan Ou asked, grumbling as she forced her way to her tired feet. "Is it just in a line, or is it encircling them?"

"It's a line," Pan Su said. "It shoots up miles high in the

air, as well as from side to side. The others are saying that it's similar to the great wall the Bone People first called up, when they invaded."

The wonder on his face made Gan Ou roll her eyes. Pan Su was still too young. He couldn't understand the implications of such an act. All he saw was the amazing skill it took to create such a large edifice.

He might be learning how to be stubborn from being with an old person like her, but he didn't grasp how to be sneaky. Not yet. Possibly not ever. It wasn't in the straight-forward nature of the Wind People.

"The Bone People are trying to get away," Gan Ou told him.

The younger person shook his head. "Really? Why would they do that?"

"We killed so many of them when their line broke and they started running away at the end of today's battle," Gan Ou pointed out. "Plus, they don't want to negotiate. It's all or nothing with the Bone People." Their greed made it impossible for them to envision sharing resources, magic, anything with anyone.

"So they're just leaving?" Pan Su said.

"Eh. Probably," Gan Ou said. "Let's go to the tent of the elders. See what they have to say."

It was a good thing that Pan Su had awoken her, as Gan Ou had no doubt that the elders would be calling for her next. At least this way she was somewhat prepared, able to force her tired old wits to start working before she had to speak in front of them.

As Gan Ou and Pan Su made their way through the camp, toward the elders' tent, a messenger came running up.

"Good, you're awake," he said, bowing his head toward her. "The elders would speak with you. Come."

Pan Su shot Gan Ou a worried look.

Gan Ou turned to him and rattled off two dozen names, those who had the strongest winds and were the most able to control them.

"Fetch them quickly," she said. "Go on. I'll be fine."

It warmed Gan Ou's heart how the members of her cohort appeared to worry about her, trying to take care of her, protect her from the elders.

Did she need their protection? She wasn't certain. The elders certainly had never threatened her, and they seemed to appreciate the help she'd given them. They'd never mentioned trying to banish her again.

Even if her staying meant that she was teaching their children how to kill.

The guards standing on either side of the opening of the tent of the elders pulled it aside as she came hobbling up, so that Gan Ou could enter immediately. It looked much the same as the last time she'd seen it, with a large fire in the center of the room, the smoke magically directed out an opening in the middle of the roof. Cots were places along the walls, and benches for the elders had been set just past the fire.

She gritted her teeth so she wouldn't point out that the rest of them, that is, the ones actually doing the fighting, slept on the cold dirt.

The elders paid Gan Ou the courtesy of a bench on her side of the fire, that she dropped down onto heavily. She couldn't help but yawn mightily as she did so.

She was an old woman, damn it! She needed her sleep. Couldn't they wait until morning to find out what mischief the Bone People were causing?

Hi Lop stood up to talk. She still retained that air of impeccable serenity, while the others around her had faded with the continued war. They all had more lines in their faces, the fighting having aged them all. Though none of them looked as though they felt as old as she did, as if they didn't fully realize just how much healing the Wind People would need after the war.

"Something happened last night with the Bone People," Hi Lop said.

Gan Ou nodded. Everyone knew that.

"What, we cannot say. I know some think that their king has been killed, but I would assume that they had an heir in place, so it wouldn't have affected this group so significantly. I believe that something else occurred, something that was truly beyond their reckoning."

"What do you think it was?" Gan Ou asked, curious. Hi Lop might have heard something that she had yet to share with the rest of the camp.

Not that the elder was about to tell Gan Ou the gossip. No, Gan Ou wasn't an equal or an elder. She was just an old woman to be ordered around.

"I believe they've suffered some sort of massive defeat elsewhere," Hi Lop said. "Something that would leave all of their people drained. We know that the priests can connect them in battle, pull upon the strength of their fighters to do greater magics. More than one elder has suggested that all the Bone People are connected somehow. And that the blow that struck them last night has drained their warriors of their vitality."

"And yet, they called up a great wall again, to hide behind," Gan Ou said.

"We need to see what's occurring on the other side of the wall," Hi Lop said.

"Consider it done," Gan Ou said, standing. She paused, waiting, as the elders looked at each other, quick words being tossed to one another on the winds.

"Is there anything else?" Gan Ou asked after a moment.

"No, no, that would be all," Hi Lop said, her face perfectly blank.

Gan Ou opened her mouth then shut it again. She wasn't tired enough—yet—to remind the elders of their manners, that a "thank you" would take them far.

She wasn't there to teach them manners. Her job was to teach the children to be deadly.

It was up to Gan Ou and her cohort to do the dirty work. Things the elders could deny, keeping their high and mighty place in the loose hierarchy of the Wind People.

Pan Su waited just outside the tent. "What did they want?" he asked.

"Where are the others?" Gan Ou said.

"They're gathering at your campfire," Pan Su said.

Gan Ou nodded and started walking back that way, holding her tongue until they arrived. Someone had lit the fire again, adding wood to the coals so that the light danced high. The smell of clean smoke made her smile, overtaking the scent of the old fires that had destroyed Shan Yu.

A circle of the strongest Wind mages stood around the fire, silent and grim.

"The Bone People have set up another wall," Gan Ou said without preamble. "I'm assuming that they're trying to hide something behind it. They know that we won't let it stand for very long. They know that the first thing we'll do is to blow it down. This means they have traps set. You will have to be careful. We can't just go blowing that damned thing apart. There will be nasty shit just on the other side of the wall."

The others nodded as they took in her words. They were just children. So young and innocent. Gan Ou knew that the eldest who stood in the group with her were barely in their twenties. They'd grown up fast during the war.

They didn't understand sneaky, though.

Lucky for them, Gan Ou had spent decades with the Stone People, who knew how to hide and dissemble, for all their practicality.

"How long is the wall?" Gan Ou asked.

"Several miles," Pan Su said. "Scouts actually haven't found either end of it, yet. Or haven't sent word back if they have."

Gan Ou grunted. That surprised her. She'd expected the wall to be more local.

Maybe the stupid Bone People only knew how to build a great big one and couldn't do something small.

Either that, or there was a really nasty surprise waiting for the Wind People on the other side.

"Divide yourselves into teams of three," Gan Ou said, coming to a decision. She wasn't about to risk all of her group. Smaller teams would hopefully mean fewer deaths. "Those with the most control go first. Not the strongest," she warned. She didn't want her strongest Wind mages to be knocked out or killed immediately. Those with the most amount of control could make more precise cuts through the wall, as well as be able to calm their winds the quickest.

"Each team has their spot on the wall. Space yourselves apart, maybe thirty feet or more between groups. When you hear the signal, the first member of your team starts their winds, pushing through the wall, tearing it apart. Stop as soon as you get to the far side."

"And the others in the team?" someone asked.

"You're backup. Be ready to rescue the first member from whatever is on the other side. Pick them up with your winds and carry them away. Do not expose yourself to it if at all possible."

"What is on the other side of the wall?" another person asked.

Gan Ou shrugged. "Just traps if we're lucky. The abyss, if we're not."

Though the group gathered around Gan Ou were already grim, that appeared to put an additional damper on them.

Good. She wanted them paranoid as well as prepared for the worst.

Hopefully, the wall was merely a distraction so that the Bone People could escape and run away.

Gan Ou didn't figure she'd ever be that lucky.

THE WALL that Gan Ou faced was different than the one she'd seen before. This one was dryer. It was composed of more smoke, less mist. Did that mean there were actual fires on the other side?

She hadn't forgotten the smell of all that smoke, though. There were more ashes in this wall as well. A line of white spots littered the base of it. It had its own glow, a blank white that stretched forever to the sides as well as up. Her stomach knotted with the memory of crossing the damned thing so many times, trying to rescue the prisoners that the Bone People had ensnared.

It surprised Gan Ou that she didn't smell magic in the wall. Was that because this wall had a physical base? Had it been created out of smoke and not mist? She didn't know.

One of Gan Ou's team members transformed into a large goose and took off, flying down the line and honking loudly, giving the signal that it was time to start attacking the wall.

Pan Su had tried to insist that Gan Ou not be the one going through the wall first, that she shouldn't risk herself that way. She'd laughed in his face. She could risk herself any way she saw fit.

The young person just didn't understand stubborn. Plus,

she'd always wanted to try her winds against one of the Bone People's walls. She'd been dreaming about since she'd first discovered them.

Gan Ou did follow her own advice. She penetrated the wall slowly, parting the wall in front of her carefully as she stepped forward. The smoke slid easily to either side of her. Ash whirled around her, blinding her. She felt her way by touch, the ground beneath her guiding her.

The first wall had felt so cold, and carried the iron smell of winter. This one was warm by comparison, like standing at the edge of a huge bonfire and the wind blowing the hot smoke. The smell of magic came about halfway through, that smell of burnt sugar that coated the back of her throat, making her gag.

Gan Ou pushed her winds ahead of her as she felt the wall thinning. It was at least one hundred paces thick. The other side felt more permeable, as if it was just made up of thin fog.

After pausing for a moment, Gan Ou pushed her winds up high. Whatever was on the other side of the wall was probably waiting for her on the ground. She considered transforming for a moment, but decided against it. She couldn't call any winds when she was wearing anything other than her Wind Person form.

With a slight *pop*, Gan Ou pushed through the other side.

An oily darkness flowed around her. It was like those damned clouds that the priests generated, that sapped the will of the Wind People. She immediately tried to push the inky substance away with her winds.

However, these clouds clung to her winds. Instead of pushing the awful conjured smoke of the Bone People away, her winds grew infected with the black abyss.

Gan Ou calmed her winds immediately, her breathing

rough, fear spiking through her, making her shiver in the cold.

If she'd come blasting through the wall, the darkness of the Bone People would have spread wide and far.

Were her people doing the same? Damn it! They should have waited until morning when they would have at least been able to see what was going on.

Gan Ou blew a hurried word back to Pan Su, telling him of the darkness and for the Wind People to stop their assault. Then she took to the air, flying to the closest group.

The lead person in the next group had made the same decision as Gan Ou and had stopped her assault early.

The third group wasn't so lucky. All three people in the team were choking on the black abyss that had been waiting for them on the other side, coughing and unable to breathe. Gan Ou wasn't sure what to do for them. She kept her winds swirling tightly around them, isolating them while trying to bleed off some of the oily cloud. It was hard work keeping such precise control on her winds. She felt whatever energy she'd had from her disturbed sleep draining out of her.

It wouldn't be until much later that the Wind People realized that the oily substance dove straight into their lungs, crippling them for the rest of their lives.

Of the eight teams, only three ended up sick. It could have been much, much worse. The trap left behind by the Bone People could have been so easily spread by the Wind People, cast up into the air for everyone nearby to breathe.

Why hadn't they thrown up this defense before? Gan Ou had to assume that the Bone People were just as vulnerable to the attack. Calling forth this darkness would be a plague on both their Peoples. It wasn't worth the risk earlier.

Gan Ou made sure that others took care of the sick ones, carrying them to healers.

Then, she and those remaining tried to disarm the black

river of clouds that ran along the edge of where the fog wall had been. No one was allowed to cross it for fear of being infected. It took them two days to clear out the path, to scrub the air clear of the darkness. It was tricky work. They couldn't just blow the darkness away, no, it would congregate someplace else. They buried some of it, the ground appearing to absorb it better. But most of it they actually had to wash away, bringing water in long lines of buckets.

Of course, by the time the Wind People were finally able to get through the clouds of darkness, the Bone People were long gone.

They could catch them. They could transform into animals that traveled much faster than the elk. But what good would that do? They didn't want to kill all the Bone People who'd been fighting. They just wanted the Bone People to leave them alone. They'd succeeded in that.

An uneasy quiet lay over the camp of the army, which Gan Ou ignored. Instead, she was grateful for the rest, and spent the next day sleeping.

Finally, the elders announced victory. They'd won the war. It didn't feel like much of a win, with their enemy skulking away in the dead of night, leaving booby traps behind. But victory it was.

People started to say their goodbyes, packing up their meager goods, getting ready to head home. They held a huge ceremony that night. The priests and priestesses sanctified one of the battlefields so that people could dance.

Gan Ou danced a little, but spent most of the night sitting beside one of the campfires. She told tales of those who had been most brave, sharing her tears with those who would listen.

Pan Su sat beside her. "Where will you go?" he asked during one of the lulls.

Gan Ou shrugged. "Don't know. I want to stay here, in

the lands of the Wind People. I don't want to go back to Killapany."

Pan Su nodded. "The latest rumor is that the Stone People are still occupied by the Bone People."

"I'm tired of fighting," Gan Ou said with a sigh. She turned to Pan Su. "Do you think we should go and help the Stone People?"

He paused, thoughtful. "Maybe. But there's a chance that the Bone People there also suffered the same sort of setbacks as the army here. They may have already pulled back." He nodded, as if coming to some sort of decision for himself. "If they haven't, if the next messenger says that the Stone People are still in serious trouble, I will go to help."

Gan Ou smiled. Pan Su felt sort of like the son she'd never had. She was glad that he'd made the right decision, even if it meant being separated from him.

"But I think you should stay here," Pan Su said after a moment, as if anticipating where her own thoughts were leading her. "You've done enough. More than enough."

"Is it enough?" she asked. "Will it ever be enough?"

"The elders will never trust you," Pan Su said, bluntly honest. "But you don't need them. You have your own followers who will support you in anything that you do."

"So you're saying I should form my own village?" Gan Ou asked with a sly smile. "Where I rule?"

Pan Su tilted his head from side to side. "Maybe not a village or a town," he said. "But a school."

"Who would come and learn from me?" Gan Ou said, dismissing the idea.

Pan Su merely gave her a look, which told her plainly how foolish he thought she was being.

Of course, there would be Wind People who would want to learn how to form their own winds. Maybe she could teach them to just use the gentle, delicate winds, and not the ones that killed.

"Maybe," she said after a few moments. It sounded nice, though. A school, off in its own village. Surrounded by trees. No major road leading to it. You had to know how to get there, or be invited. With a huge meadow off to one side, where the children could practice.

Yes, she could see it.

But Gan Ou knew better than to have hopes or dreams.

Particularly when Ka Lem arrived the next morning with news.

Chapter Eight

STONE

NOALANON STOOD with the rest of her group in the tunnel under the temple, waiting for the signal that they should start their attack. The air felt stuffy and was filled with the smell of dust and sand. The cramped enclosure felt hot, despite how they each could control their own internal temperature. No words were exchanged—three dozen Stone People waited as still as the rocks around them. It was as silent as a tomb.

The walls around them trembled. In the distance, Noalanon heard a soft *wuff.*

That was it. The first wall surrounding the temple complex had fallen.

The Stone People came barreling out of the tunnel, moving quickly. A loud growl filled the room they entered, carried along with them.

It hadn't occurred to Noalanon that this group was the most angry of any of them.

Instead of destroying the door, the first to reach the surface started pushing through the walls. They were determined to do as much damage to this building as they possibly could. Most of the guards would now be outside the buildings, dealing with the crowds that surrounded them.

There wasn't any real trick to knocking down a wall. Noalanon merely placed zir hands on the cool stone in front of zir and pushed. It was partly strength that worked in zir favor, but partly zir affinity toward the rock. The wall gave way before zir, a large hole appearing where ze'd been pushing just a moment before.

It didn't take long for zir to kick zir way through to the next room, which turned out to be a study of some sort, with desks.

Had it been used by the priests? Keeping track of their experiments?

Ze dropped zir elbows on a desk, the mere wood giving way to mighty stone with a loud crack.

Only then did Noalanon turned to the left, heading toward the door. Zir smaller sub-group was supposed to get to the tower, which was in another area of the temple complex. The priests would be gathered there, belching out their filth, trying to control the Stone People, maybe getting them to turn against one another.

Zir group didn't have any builders with them. They all just had the understanding that if enough of the internal walls of the building collapsed, so would the building.

No one had actually anticipated what it would feel like when the roof dropped down on their heads. Only a soft groan had warned zir of the coming demise. Then tiles and walls collapsed, solid stone bruising Noalanon's side.

They learned later that the crush of the roof had killed most of the Bone People who'd stayed inside the first building.

Some of the Stone People were trapped by the falling debris, or, as in the case of Noalanon, momentarily pushed over until ze could free zirself. Ze was slightly bruised, not scratched or bleeding. Startled rather than hurt.

Ze helped free the half dozen ze'd started with, from fallen walls and roof tiles. The air was thick with dust.

They kicked their way out of the remains of the building, into the dusty courtyard beyond.

Guards rushed at them. Noalanon bared zir teeth at them but kept walking toward the center tower. A weighted net fell over Noalanon. Ze growled loudly, spiking zir internal temperature, burning the rope away, the smell of ash filling the air. When a guard came up and tried to stab zir with a knife, Noalanon felt zir temper snap. Ze didn't try to punch the guard in the face. Instead, ze used zir arm like a bat, swinging angrily.

Though the guard ducked, he didn't drop his head down far enough. Noalanon hit the side of his head hard with zir forearm. The guard fell to the ground abruptly.

Noalanon stomped down on the fallen body, zir foot connecting solidly with the guard's chest. The sound of breaking bones was incredibly loud as well as satisfying. Ze carefully took aim, them stomped down twice more, breaking the guard's arms.

The guard didn't even jerk as ze injured him.

Had ze killed him with zir first strike? Ze didn't know, and didn't care.

The first group of guards was quickly demolished, and Noalanon and zir group hurried on to the tower that stood in the center of the temple complex.

More guards stood there. They fought fiercely, stabbing and kicking, throwing nets and trying to knock down the Stone People.

They didn't stand a chance. They didn't understand that it would never be a fair fight, one Bone Person against one

Stone Person. The guards' only hope was for all of them to gang up on a single Stone Person.

But that would leave them vulnerable to the rest of the attackers.

Again, Noalanon wasn't certain of the state of the guard ze had struck. Ze left him behind zir as ze approached the base of the temple.

Priests stood at the top of the open tower, pouring out their filth. Noalanon raised zir body temperature a little more, then started zir own holy work, tearing down the false god that they'd allowed into their midst.

"Make the rock stronger as you push!"

Noalanon didn't understand what that meant in the least. Ze turned zir head while ze kept pushing, finding Hirshamin standing beside zir.

"Here," the builder said impatiently. Ze put zir hands on the wall and did…something. Noalanon could tell that the rock under zir hands was suddenly more solid. Instead of being made out of individual stones impeccably fitted together, the wall had melted together into a single piece.

"Now push!" Hirshamin instructed them. "I'll weaken the other side. That way, the tower will fall away from you. Not on top of you."

Ah. That made much more sense.

Noalanon found it more taxing to try to push such a solid wall, as opposed to pushing through the rocks, knocking them out of alignment. But ze wasn't alone. The Stone People on either side of zir added their strength.

The creaking of the tower rang out ominously over the shouts and cries of the battle all around them. Winds rushed around them, urging them to continue, carrying the fresh scent of the holy mountain. Noalanon's muscles strained as ze worked, zir arms starting to shake.

"Push!" Hirshamin directed.

Noalanon found zir feet slipping. Ze reached down with zir toes, digging deeply into the earth, finding a solid place to take a stand. Ze felt zirself grow stubborn as ze strained.

Ze was not going anyplace. This tower would move before ze did.

The stones above zir head creaked again, louder.

Something hard struck Noalanon's back. Ze grunted in pain and continued zir work. Seemed the guards had gotten smarter and were using their arrows.

However, the temple walls had been torn down in too many places. Hoards of Stone People had poured into the gaps. Noalanon heard more shrieks and cries of pain from the guards as they were dealt with.

It warmed zir heart. Ze hadn't been the only one who had had enough. No guilt arrived to sour the taste of victory.

With a final grinding screech, the stones under Noalanon's hands gave way. The tower fell with a loud crash. The ground buckled under Noalanon's feet as stone plummeted to the ground. Huge plumes of dust rose into the air, making the immediate area hazy.

Noalanon started coughing as ze made zir way to the side, out of the debris. Ze bent over, wheezing. Zir back muscles started to let zir know how little they appreciated all the strain they'd experienced that morning.

With a final shake of zir head, Noalanon straightened up, clearing zir eyes. It didn't matter what ze currently felt like. Buildings in the temple complex still stood. As did sections of the wall.

Ze wouldn't rest until it was all reduced to rubble.

THE MORNING AFTER THE BATTLE, Noalanon didn't know that ze could hurt in so many places, all at the same time. All of zir joints ached. Zir muscles sang a constant chorus of complaint, even when ze was just sitting, not moving. Zir skin was tender to the touch. The smell of dust still clogged zir nose. Ze heard a soft wind playing outside, and the murmur of the children in the kitchen.

Noalanon still lay in bed, Jolapen curled up on zir side, facing away from Noalanon. Jolapen had held Noalanon most of the night, wrapped around zir, keeping zir warm. Their cozy bedroom had never felt so much like a sanctuary. Noalanon was reluctant to leave. The day had grown brighter outside the window, though, and ze had things to do.

The Stone People had won. Most of the priests were dead. The few who'd survived were all in dark rooms, without windows, isolated from each other by thick walls. They would be unable to communicate with anyone else using their clouds.

Forni—King Einar—had also been killed. He'd been in the tower with the priests and fallen to his death with the others. Noalanon had understood that the Stone People had wanted to take him alive if possible, so that they would have an obvious head of state to negotiate with. However, his passing didn't bother zir too much.

Today, the council would meet. The two councilmembers who'd been taken over by the Bone People had finally found their own wills. However, no one trusted them. The city would hold emergency elections in the next couple of weeks.

Plus, they had to replace Sugaoshi, who'd been killed during the attack. Noalanon found the death toll staggering —over two hundred of zir people dead. At least that many of the Bone People had been killed as well. The temple had been completely destroyed. The Stone People had taken their anger out on the remains, stomping down on the stone blocks, shattering the rock until it was mere piles of pebbles and shards.

Zir people had never been killers. Murders were infrequent, though accidents did occur. Almost everyone died of sickness or old age. To have so many returned to Ishkra before their time was difficult to accept, even if they had all died as heroes.

"How are you?" came the whispered words from beside Noalanon.

"Sorry, didn't meant to wake you up," Noalanon replied, reaching for Jolapen, snuggling up again in zir arms as ze turned over.

"It's all right. Maybe I'll catch a nap later," Jolapen said. "I'm just glad that you're here. That the nightmare is finally finished."

Noalanon held zir tongue. The nightmare wasn't over, not yet. There was still so much work to do in order to heal zir people. Ze would admit that the darkness was finally receding. That much was true. But that was all.

"Thank you," Noalanon murmured, kissing Jolapen's chest. "Thank you for being here. For being my bedrock."

Jolapen kissed Noalanon's head. "Always," ze murmured.

Noalanon suddenly wished that every muscle didn't hurt as badly as it did. Ze could use some intimacy with zir partner. But even the thought of it made zir wince.

"Soon," Jolapen said with a chuckle, leaning zir head down to kiss Noalanon.

"Soon," Noalanon promised, taking a deep breath and cuddling with zir mate, taking a little while longer to relax until the day and zir children intruded.

THE COUNCILMEMBER CHAMBERS were far too small to bring together everyone who wanted to watch. Instead, the Stone People gathered in the main city square, a few blocks away from the council chambers. The morning was hazy—primarily from the dust thrown up the day before, pulling down the temple walls. The sun still shone down hot, and Noalanon found zirself adjusting zir internal temperature down more than once. At least the heat let zir forget now and again just how much ze hurt, how stiffly ze moved. That morning ze'd eaten the special minerals that had been set aside for zir and all the fighters, rich brown minerals that slid right down with green tea, as well as bitter and crunchy blue ones.

In some ways, the meeting today reminded zir of the day ze had left, so many months ago, when the five carts of travelers had gathered here. However, at that time the square had been mostly empty, as many of the travelers had said their goodbyes privately, and few had families gathered to see them off.

Noalanon wasn't certain of the last time ze had seen so many Stone People in a group. While the religious festivals for Kiproary in midsummer would bring a lot of people out, it was nothing like this. Stone People were crammed together in the square. Every window in the surrounding buildings was overflowing with the heads of onlookers, and more than one group had found their way to the nearby rooftops.

Normally, when such a large contingent of Stone People came together, there was the sound of something sifting in the background. As if rocks were brushing off one another politely, mere dust being knocked off.

Today, the sound was much harsher. More like grinding. Ze found zirself shifting from one foot to the other in angry anticipation.

Most of the Stone People around zir appeared to share zir rage. They'd been trapped under a foreign power for months. The damned priests who had disregarded or tried to change the very nature of the Stone People. She'd heard that many tea shops had thrown open their doors all night, and that more than one impromptu party had occurred in the main market, the Stone People happy to be allowed out in the evening again.

Jolapen and their three children stood next to Noalanon. Despite how much every muscle ached, Noalanon had insisted on joining with everyone else, as well as bringing the children.

History was being made. Ze wanted zir children to be able to boast that they had been there.

A large platform had been hastily assembled on the northern side of the square, the rock pillars holding up the wooden top roughly sculpted. The surviving councilmembers would stand on it, so that people might have a chance to see them. The placement of the platform had been very deliberate. It was in the exact same spot the Bone People priests had gathered during the celebrations of Kiproary, something Noalanon was just as glad that ze had missed. A grand view of the holy mountain rose up just behind where the councilmembers would stand.

Noalanon and the others who had spearheaded the attack were granted a spot close to the platform so that they could see and hear everything. While the twins seemed overly awed that their Mana had done something so important, the youngest was doing zir best to act as if these accolades were normal. Seven going on seventeen.

Hirshamin was also there with zir two sets of twins. One set looked very similar to the builder, with stocky shoulders and solid limbs. The other set had more the look of their Baba, who stood at least a head over Hirshamin and was slender, almost to the point of being willowy.

"We did it," Hirshamin said quietly to Noalanon as they waited.

Noalanon shook zir head. "We directed them. They did it," ze said, indicating the crowd around them.

Their group wouldn't have gotten as far as they had without the support of the rest of the city. There had been reports of some of the Stone People trying to defend the Bone People, particularly the Stone People who'd been employed as guards. They'd been gently stopped and were now being treated like young children who didn't know any better, who couldn't yet take care of themselves. Nutritional specialists were working with them, trying to find combinations of minerals that would help, as well as these people's partners and friends, seeking the connection that might ground them.

Finally, Juhala walked out onto the platform, followed by Yagakilly. The two other members, Mahletik and Kinrahsy, were a few steps behind.

It hurt Noalanon's heart that Sugaoshi wasn't standing up there with them. Ze had suffered so much. All ze had wanted to do was to go paint some more.

A great roar went through the crowd. It took Noalanon a moment to see that three of the Bone People priests had been brought up onto the platform. Ze knew that more than that had survived the battle. Hopefully they hadn't found their own way to Ishkra's waters.

The priests all looked dazed. Their hands were tied in front of them, bound in mere leather, not chains. Their mouths were bound as well, so that they couldn't speak, couldn't cast any of their magic or spew any of their filth.

The anger of the crowd remained even as the sound died down. It seethed around Noalanon, like a volcano ready to erupt. The rage added a sharp tang to the air, like a tea made from the first bitter greens.

"People of Killapany!" Yagakilly said, stepping forward. The representative of the merchants wore a golden brown shirt that Noalanon was certain was made from the finest material, as always. Juhala wore zir typical light gray shirt with darker gray skirt, more utilitarian than dressy. Both Mahletik and Kinrahsy wore rich black vests over fine white shirts and dark green pants, but weren't in their finest clothes. Maybe they were trying to appear humble, contrite for what they'd done, even if they hadn't had their full will at the time.

"Today we are gathered together to remember those who lost their lives in the battle for our freedom!" Yagakilly said. Zir words were followed by a loud roar from the crowd, unable to contain their feelings.

Noalanon shivered. Ze had never heard zir people be so loud.

"We recognize those who have led us here," Yagakilly said. Ze indicated the area where Noalanon, Hirshamin, and the others stood. Ze called out their names, though half of them were drowned out by the cheering of the crowd.

Noalanon smiled but still felt bemused. Ze was no hero. As Jolapen had said, there had been an injustice. Ze had seen it corrected. That was all.

Yagakilly finally got the crowd settle again. "We will celebrate those who led us to victory over the next few weeks. As well as have a proper celebration for Kiproary."

Zir words brought a stillness over the crowd. As one, all the Stone People threw their gaze up to the holy mountain. It shone so brightly, even with the haze. It finally seemed to calm the Stone People and they remembered their place, the deep reservoirs of solid strength that lay under their feet.

After a few moments of silence, Yagakilly drew all attention back towards zir.

"We have lost many of our People," Yagakilly said solemnly. "Sugaoshi, our fellow councilmember, for one."

The quality of the air changed subtly, going from joyous to expectant.

"There will be general elections in the next two weeks," Juhala said. "As we will need to replace three members of the council."

Mahletik and Kinrahsy nodded. While Noalanon suspected they might want to stay in power, they knew that their positions were untenable. They had to resign. No one would truly trust them again.

"But before then, we have a decision to make, as a People," Yagakilly said.

The three priests were brought forward.

An angry growl greeted them. Noalanon was close enough to see that even as pale as the Bone People's skin was, they could grow much whiter.

Good. She'd promised to teach them fear.

"Has there been enough killing?" Yagakilly asked.

Juhala stepped forward, obviously taking the other side. "Or not enough?" ze called out over the crowd.

The crowd seemed to take a deep collective breath.

Noalanon took a deep breath as well. Zir tired body still complained about zir standing there instead of resting. Ze wasn't sure ze had the ability to form cohesive thoughts with the exhaustion pounding at the back of zir skull, sending find tremors down the backs of zir legs.

Yagakilly continued. "The Bone People will never be allowed to cross any of our borders again," ze proclaimed. "Hirshamin and the others can awaken stones there, that will warn us if any of them try to cross. They will not be able to return. I say that we drop all of the Bone People who remain on the far side of these stones, with instructions to return to their People with the news. Carry our message that they are never to return."

Noalanon shook zir head, a soft growl in zir throat. Didn't they realize that wouldn't work? What was the news from the Wind People? The Sea People? Just getting rid of the Bone People in the lands of the Stone People wasn't enough.

Juhala spoke up. "The Bone People have caused grievous harm not just to us, but to all the Peoples."

Noalanon found zirself nodding. Yes.

"We need to deal not just with the group who remains here, but with all the Bone People. Just killing those here isn't enough. We need to permanently keep the Bone People away from all of our lands," Juhala said.

Fear took hold of Noalanon. Crap. That meant more war, far away in the lands of the Bone People.

The same fear appeared to have spread over the rest of the crowd. They understood the implications of what Juhala was saying. A ripple of silence followed as the Stone People considered the choices ahead of them.

Closing their own borders would never be enough.

Anger, fear, and dread sounded in the voices that called out. Some did shout that all they needed to do was to make their borders aware. And Noalanon was certain that would be done regardless of whatever was done here.

The vote wasn't precise. No one issued ballots or bothered counting heads.

The will of the people, through the overwhelming noise they made, was clear.

The Stone People would go to war against all of the Bone People.

They would all learn fear.

NOALANON ATE dinner that night with just zir family. The twins chatted away amiably about their friends and what they were planning on doing for the next few days, until school resumed. The kitchen booth they all sat in felt cozy and warm, the slightly sweet smell of the minerals they consumed in the air. The golden light hanging over the table shone like a blessing.

It all was so normal and familiar, and yet, Noalanon felt as though something was still off, as if ze struggled half a step behind the rest of them and could never quite catch up.

Mathigorn, the youngest, sat quietly. Finally, just as they were finishing up, ze turned zir big blue eyes up at Noalanon and asked, "Are you going to leave again, Mana?"

Silence dropped like a heavy weight all around them. Noalanon realized that all of them had the same question, that they'd all been waiting for some sort of announcement from zir.

"I don't know," Noalanon said. "There are plenty of others who could also do this work," ze said, trying to give some comfort to zir child.

"But there's still an injustice being done," Turkastein said. Ze exchanged a glance with zir twin, then continued, obviously chosen to be the one to speak at this point. "Baba said that you had to go because of that."

"I know," Noalanon said. "And I may end up being one of those who leaves. But I may not be." Ze sighed. "I don't ever want to leave home again," ze admitted.

Jolapen reached across the table and squeezed Noalanon's hand. "We'll support you. Whatever you decide."

Mathigorn rolled zir eyes. "Maybe the rest of us should leave for a while so that you two can reconnect."

The twins snickered.

Noalanon deliberately threw a kiss Jolapen's way with zir other hand. "I need to connect with my partner, yes," ze said. Ze squeezed Jolapen's hand one last time, then let go. "But I also want to spend time with my family. To be with all of you. You're why I went to do what I did."

Ze paused, then added, "You are also the reason why I

would leave again, if I had to. I would do anything to keep you safe. So that you could grow up and raise up your own children without fear."

The twins nodded. Mathigorn gave Noalanon a cool, appraising look. "Everyone has to be safe from the black clouds," ze said solemnly. "Not just us."

Seven going on seventeen, indeed.

"No, not just us," Noalanon agreed. "But I don't have to decide tonight. No one does. We've sent messengers to the Wind People, as well as the Sea People, to let them know what happened here. The Sea People are still safe. It's the Wind People we're most worried about."

The latest news had been that the Wind People were fighting terrible battles against an army of Bone People, slowly making their way across the Wind People's lands.

"We'll stop them," Mathigorn said fiercely.

"We will," Noalanon promised, realizing that yes, ze might have to leave again.

Even if it was the last thing ze wanted to do.

Chapter Nine

SEA

THOUGH LISETH WAS GENERALLY in better control of her reactions, she couldn't help her verbal clicks when she learned that Ajooless had reached out to communicate again, after all these weeks. Liseth thanked Ishkra for her own foresight, to always have someone waiting at the side of the fountain, in case Ajooless did use the fish again.

Sasuelana sat quietly in Liseth's office once she finished relating her news. Her creamy blue-white skin seemed slightly pale, particularly contrasted with her sage green gown.

Liseth still considered her office her sanctuary, despite its utilitarian nature. It certainly wasn't as fancy as the office of her former counterpart, Bayaseth. Still, she liked the way the sunlight struck the plain gray-stone floor, the organized mess of books, scrolls, and knickknacks on the shelves that covered every wall, and the fresh irises she'd chosen that morning for the altar to Ishkra that stood in the corner.

"Have you ever heard of someone sharing as Ajooless did, spitting out her local waters so that the receiver on the other end would know exactly where the sender was?" Liseth asked. It wasn't in any myth that she'd ever heard of.

"No, my lady," Sasuelana said. Before she'd come to see Liseth, she'd gone to the trackers in the temple, carrying the water Ajooless had shared. They had said they could use it for tracking, that it greatly shortened their search. The Sea People would know the exact location of the home waters of the Bone People in the next day or so.

"We will have to make sure that it is added to the myth of Ajooless," Liseth said.

Sasuelana nodded, a big smile overtaking her face, showing just how beautiful she could look. "Aye," she said. "The girl needs her own myth." Then Sasuelana grew serious again. "But what about the other part of her message?"

Liseth sighed. "I don't know," she said truthfully. Did they want to try and bring another plague forward? Particularly since so many had died from the catastrophe of the most recent one?

"Would you like my straightforward counsel?" Sasuelana asked.

Liseth clicked again, surprised. Sasuelana had never, not once in all the years that Liseth had known her, been straightforward. Instead, her assistant had always been a master manipulator, not allowing Liseth to see how she was being maneuvered until very recently.

"Yes, I would," Liseth said cautiously. Why did this feel like as much of a trap as anything else Sasuelana did?

"I would do exactly as Ajooless suggested," Sasuelana said. "Whatever plague we cause won't work exactly as we mean it to. You and I already know that, though we shouldn't spell that out for the others. There are far too many variables. And it will mutate. However, it will also keep the damned Bone People weak for generations. We need that breathing space in order to rebuild."

"Is that how you would have me argue before the council of regents?" Liseth said, finally hiding her surprise for the first time that afternoon. She honestly had expected Sasuelana to argue for saving the Bone People, not to send them a plague that would sterilize a large portion of their population.

Or maybe Liseth hadn't been as successful as she'd thought, given the sly smile that Sasuelana gave her in response. "I would have you say whatever it takes to get the regents to agree with your point of view," Sasuelana said. "The Bone People are evil. And greedy. They must be stopped. Or the third age will end in flames. It will be the will of the gods."

Liseth sighed. "Are we just delaying the end of the third age? Not preventing it?"

Sasuelana started laughing. "I forget, sometimes, that you have no offspring," she managed to say between loud giggles

Liseth found her back stiffening, sitting up straighter in her chair. What in Ishkra's name did Sasuelana mean by that?

"All things die," Sasuelana said finally as she brought herself under better control. "If you were more in touch with children and families, you'd understand that. The third age will end, whether we will it or not. And a new age will be born. A fourth age. With its own myths and legends."

Liseth sat back in her chair, pondering Sasuelana's words. "That is not what we teach," she said after a while.

Sasuelana shrugged. "Maybe we ought to. Though I would understand why you wouldn't want to teach of a world that was forever being reborn. Some might take it into their heads that ending this age wouldn't be the worst thing in the world if a new one was guaranteed to take its place."

"True," Liseth said. Given the general fatalistic nature of the Sea People, letting them believe that their People would automatically be reborn wouldn't be smart.

"But you still think we should sterilize the Bone People? Those who have more of the Bone People blood in them?" Liseth asked.

Sasuelana met her eye with a serious, steady look of her own. "Aye. Our children's children will thank us for it."

SUCH AN IMPORTANT DECISION couldn't be made just by a majority vote among the regents. It had to be unanimous.

That the vote came back as such so quickly surprised Liseth. Though maybe it shouldn't have, as Sasuelana had given her all the arguments she needed for her case.

Now, it was time to put word to deed.

Liseth went to visit Gunnar, the Bone Person priest that they'd captured so many months ago, the next morning. Guards would go to see the rest of the imprisoned Bone People and gather samples from them.

Liseth thought she at least owed it to Gunnar to be present, though she knew she would never tell him the truth.

"Good news!" Liseth said cheerfully as she entered Gunnar's rooms. She immediately dipped her hands in the washbasin just inside the door.

"You've come to your senses and have decided to release all of us?" Gunnar said as he turned from the massive stone fireplace that took up much of one wall. His green eyes appeared more gray that morning, large and soulful, possibly due to the dark gray shirt he wore. He had his red-blond hair down around his thin face, framing it like a mane. His smile looked brittle. Being imprisoned had aged him severely, carved harsh lines across his broad forehead, as well as down the sides of his face. He seemed so much weaker than he'd first appeared, as if he were in his seventies instead of his forties. Or maybe that was because he had no others to draw upon, and this was actually his true age and strength.

Liseth shrugged. "More or less," she said. "You will be escorted to our borders, and we will enact protections to stop you from coming into our lands again."

"How?" Gunnar asked obviously surprised.

"We need a sample of your waters," Liseth said. She nodded at the guard waiting just outside the open door. "You will need to spit into one globe, and urinate into another. We are taking similar waters from all of the Bone People we have captured. Using these samples, we should be able to make our rivers and streams all aware of your kind."

Liseth was lying about the entire thing, but she had no reason to tell Gunnar the truth, that one of the secretive plague bringers had asked for such samples in order to fine tune the plague she was crafting.

Gunnar nodded, obviously fascinated. "And what does that mean?" he asked. He seemed wary.

How much did he know about the River People? How mixed was his blood? How much did he know, or guess, about the Sea People's true powers?

"We don't know if we can turn our waters poisonous to you," Liseth said. "But the waters will warn us if any of your kind cross our borders. Hunters and guards will be sent out immediately. And they will kill all of you."

Gunnar seemed skeptical. "Really?"

Liseth paused, considering. "Come here. Let me show you." She knew that the River People hadn't had such power. Then again, they only had a land form, not a sea form. She walked back to the basin of water close to the door and stuck both of her hands in. She kept them submerged and reached for her water form.

Hunters could maintain both their land and sea forms at the same time. They frequently would just pop their heads above the water, breathing the air while maintaining their sea form under the water.

Liseth had never tried to hold onto both before. She closed her eyes and reached for the other part of her, that side of her that felt both harder and softer.

The gasp Gunnar gave told her she'd succeeded.

When Liseth opened her eyes, she saw scales had formed across the backs of her hands. Interesting. She'd never realized how pale her skin became after the transformation. Or maybe that was just because her hands were submerged in a white bowl. She'd have to check on that at some other point. They felt the same, though, her fingers long and clever, even if webbing had formed between them. Her nails had also formed into much longer claws, sharp and deadly.

"Your eyes," Gunnar said, peering at her with horror. "They're black."

"Yes," Liseth said, though she hadn't realized that would happen. She smiled at him, showing off her now pointed teeth. "We have a true sea form," she explained, removing her hands from the water and drying them off.

The change to her full land form felt abrupt, as if she'd suddenly been blasted with hot air. She clicked once in surprise.

"We have much more control over our nearby waters than the Stone or Wind People," Liseth continued as she stepped toward the priest.

"Abomination," Gunnar whispered, taking an automatic step back. "We'd heard rumors, but nothing…"

Liseth smiled at him. "And this abomination would warn you away from all of our lands," she said clearly. "You and all your People. You will never be welcome again."

"My People will starve," Gunnar said bitterly.

"Yes, some will," Liseth said. She wasn't about to tell him that in a generation or so, their lands would be able to feed them all again. "You will survive, though. If you'd come to us in peace, we would have helped." Particularly since the Bone People and the River People's blood had mingled.

The River People would have been welcomed by the Sea People.

"We never would have been able to get our People to accept that creatures as different as you would have helped us," Gunnar admitted softly.

"You will never be welcome in our lands," Liseth repeated. She motioned the guard forward. Gunnar hesitated, but he spit obligingly into the globe that the guard handed to him. "I don't know if you'll be welcome in the Wind or Stone People's lands after this."

"But?" Gunnar said. He appeared to hear her hesitation.

"But maybe we can arrange a grand trading time, a festival, in the meadows and plains to the east of the Wind People," Liseth said. It had been an idea she'd been toying with for some time: To meet the Bone People, and their cousins the River People, during a time of peace instead of war. Send the bravest merchants, those most willing to take a risk on what could be the profit of a lifetime, bringing back unique delicacies and goods from so far away.

"I will ask, when I return to Melefels, the capital," Gunnar said. "I swear to it."

Liseth clicked, both in surprise as well as acknowledgement. "Your people will be escorted to the border in a week or so. We need a bit of time to work our magic."

Gunnar nodded. "Thank you for treating us so… hospitably," he said.

"I'm aware you wouldn't have done the same," Liseth said dryly.

"True enough," Gunnar said with a chuckle. "But I've

learned during my time here. How you might be People, despite your differences."

He stuck out a hand. Curious, Liseth took it, surprised to find that he wrapped both of his warm hands around her cool ones, holding on for a moment before letting go.

"I will see you before you leave," Liseth told him, turning away.

"If you do set up a trading festival," Gunnar said, his voice soft and low, "make sure it is on the plains. Never let any of your people go to Melefels."

"Understood," Liseth said. Ajooless had told the story of the elk.

Gunnar didn't need to know that soon enough, the Bone People would no longer be a threat. To anyone.

LISETH STOOD JUST outside the city, south of the large gate that arched over the trade road. She felt it was appropriate to say goodbye to the Bone People in the same place she'd originally met them.

Several hunters were ranged behind her. The hands of the Bone People were tied, though their mouths had been left ungagged, after Gunnar had given his word to not try to speak any magic. Hunters had javelins ready in case he decided to risk it.

The day was wet and rainy—Ishkra's further protection of the Sea People. Even if the Bone People managed to start their magic, it would never hold, not in weather such as this. Liseth raised her face to the mist, smiling as the drops caressed her skin.

After so little contact with their masters, the elk had perished. Their keepers had come out one morning to find mere piles of bones. Whatever magic had sustained the horrific creatures had drained away. Gunnar had seemed shocked when Liseth had told him. In fact, that was when he'd truly started to age.

The Bone People still had carts to draw them, but now there were small oxen pulling them, the kind favored by the merchants of the Stone People. The Bone People had been given instructions on how to care for their animals, mostly for the sake of the oxen. Liseth didn't really care if the Bone People ended up walking the entire way across all the lands going back to their own.

She had, however, given Gunnar two items in case their group met with others determined to kill them. One was a great glass globe that glowed with a bright magical light. The other was a page, written and signed by the council of regents, granting the group safe passage back to their lands.

She didn't know if either would stop anyone else from killing them. That was out of her hands. She hoped, actually, that Gunnar did make it all the way back to the capital of the Bone People, just so he could tell them that they were not welcome in the lands of the Sea People. As well as to carry the myth that the waters in the lands of the Sea People would be turned against them.

Gunnar looked even more ancient outside of the city. Liseth had hoped that being outside might bring more color to his overly pale face, but it hadn't. He stood in front of the group he led, straight and tall, though she suspected that he'd go sit in a cart as soon as they said their goodbyes.

"Thank you for your forbearance," Gunnar said, addressing Liseth. "As well as your hospitality."

"You are welcome," Liseth said, still pleased and surprised that Gunnar recognized their hospitality. They might have been friends if they'd met in different circumstances. Then she grew somber.

"You are never to return to the lands of the Sea People," Liseth said. "The Bone People are not welcome."

"Understood," Gunnar said, nodding. He paused, then gave her a smile. "May your people fare well and prosper. May the soft nights of Valtyr carry you to your fondest dreams."

"May Ishkra hold you close to her bosom, washing you in the waters of forgetting only when it is your time," Liseth replied. "May there be many years of gathering wisdom before then."

"Thank you," Gunnar said. He bowed his head, then turned and walked, stiff legged and stiff backed, over to the first cart. One of the guards helped him climb up, as Gunnar's hands were tied.

Then the group departed, heading over the hills and back the way they'd come. They'd take the southern route through the lands, the route that Ajooless and the others had originally taken. The hunters would drop them off at the border, then stay a short while to make sure that the Bone People actually continued on their way.

Could Liseth or the other Sea People make the waters of their home land aware somehow? So that her threat of turning all the waters of the Sea People against the Bone People came true? Liseth had asked others, but no one seemed to think it was possible. It was never the same water. Even lakes were fed by underground streams or aquifers. It might be possible to visit a body of water and ask who had passed recently. That would be the best that any among the Sea People could manage, however.

The plague targeted against the Bone People had already been unleashed. No one would know the effect for years. Hopefully it would work, and the threat of the Bone People would diminish.

Without bringing about the end of the third age.

LISETH WAS both thrilled and dismayed by the news from the Stone People. They'd battled the Bone People in Killapany and had won. However, they were now declaring war, and were determined to take their battles all the way into the lands of the Bone People.

"We have to stop them," Liseth told Sasuelana. They were meeting in the back garden of the temple, having brought their own sweet tea and a picnic with them. The fountain that contained the goldfish that Ajooless spoke through splashed merrily to their side. The rest of the garden was deserted—Liseth had insisted on privacy during her lunch with Sasuelana. A misting rain fell, which Liseth welcomed, feeling blessed by Ishkra.

"Why do we have to stop them?" Sasuelana asked, sounding innocent. She took another bite of the delicious seaweed cake that the temple cooks had made for them. It was held together with eggs, with crunchy seeds baked on top. It had a nutty flavor, the seaweed bringing a lovely touch of salt and earthiness to the cake.

"Because they no longer need to go to war," Liseth said. What was Sasuelana playing at? "We've taken care of the matter."

"Have we?" Sasuelana said. "We only think that we have. We don't know for certain. We won't know for many, many years. If ever."

"But we have to tell the Stone People!" Liseth said. "They will lose so many lives if we don't."

"No one outside of the Sea People actually understands all our powers," Sasuelana pointed out. "Do the Wind or Stone People realize that we can create plagues? And cast them upon any waters?"

Liseth opened her mouth then shut it again.

"I don't know. We've always denied having such magic. Instead, I've maintained the myth that the Sea People just have a weak constitution. It's why we keep getting so sick. Not because we create the plagues themselves."

Sasuelana nodded. "That's always been the policy. None of the other Peoples truly know what we can do. And we need to keep it that way."

"Even if it means allowing the Stone People to go fight in a war that is unnecessary?" Liseth asked, the words turning the delicious food in front of her bitter.

"Yes," Sasuelana said. "I understand it's galling. Imagine, though, if the Stone People understood our powers. That we could, at any time, reach out and start killing them off with plagues if we so choose."

"We would never do that!" Liseth said. "They're our allies." Particularly now, since they'd all had their own battles with the Bone People.

Sasuelana shrugged. "Our population has been shrinking. Theirs has been growing. What happens if they decide they need more of our land? What would we do to stop them?"

Liseth shuddered. She wouldn't ever want to be faced with such a decision. However, she had to admit that such a scenario was possible in a few decades.

"And you know the rumors, right? That the Stone People are able to call rocks from out of the earth. Given time, they could take over our land, make it all mountains," Sasuelana said.

"That's not true," Liseth said, dismissive of such a notion. "They can't do that."

"Just like we can't cause sickness or plagues in any water," Sasuelana said, nodding. "Or else the Wind and Stone Peoples would already know about it. Right?"

Liseth sighed. She understood Sasuelana's point. If they lied about their capacities, so would the other Peoples.

"Even though we know that they're throwing their lives away, we cannot stop the Stone People from going to war with the Bone People," Liseth said with a sigh. Such a waste.

Would this continued war be enough to bring about the end of the third age? There would be far-reaching ripples from stones dropped in those waters, even if they were far away, in a land not their own.

Sasuelana gave Liseth a sharp look. "Not only can we not prevent it, we are going to have to support it."

"And waste our own People's lives?" Liseth said. It just wasn't right.

"I don't know how many would actually go to war," Sasuelana said.

"More than you'd think," Liseth said. "Remember when I first asked for people to travel to the lands of the Wind People? Many more volunteered than we'd expected."

"True," Sasuelana said. "Though I think there won't be as many volunteers this time. A lot of the people who might have gone on such an adventure have already left for the new villages up and down the coast."

Liseth nodded. "I hadn't thought of that." Sasuelana was probably right. So many had volunteered to leave the underwater city of Sillboden, going to one of the frontier towns. Many more than Liseth or Bayaseth had initially anticipated. Plus, there had been reports of more births since they'd left, and more multiple births than there had been in the old days.

"We will have to send supplies to the Stone People, though," Sasuelana said. "Waterproof backpacks. Dried goods. And scribes who will record everything that occurs."

"Why would we send scribes?" Liseth asked, confused.

"Neither the Wind nor the Stone People train as we do," Sasuelana said. "No one else can remember things as precisely as a Sea Person. If we want there to be records of the battles and the wars, we need to be the ones doing the remembering. Surely you don't expect the Wind People to remember this war after a century."

"So instead of hunters or warriors, we offer them scribes," Liseth said thinking it through. "And we set up our own messengers. Ones who can use their powers as Ajooless has shown us." She paused, then added, "Of course, that would mean telling the rest of the Sea People that this ability was possible."

Liseth had only told the regents as well as a few trusted priestesses what Ajooless could do. It had turned out that only one other of the acolytes in the temple had been able to develop the same strange ability of talking through a fish. It appeared to be a very rare talent.

Then again, so few had tried. If more of the Sea People learned that it was possible, maybe they'd find more who could do it.

"I'm hesitant to tell all of the Sea People that the age of the heroines has returned, that these powers are available, that they should try," Sasuelana said.

"Why?" Liseth asked. "It would be useful." Surely having a string of messengers who could send them news regularly across great distances without having to travel would be to their advantage.

"Maybe. Maybe not," Sasuelana said. "Remember, Ajooless, Malyath, and now this new apprentice, can only speak through fish by draining the strength of the others around them."

"True," Liseth said. "And we know that the Bone People also have the same power."

"Or the River People did," Sasuelana said. "It's a power that we've seen abused. I hesitate to develop it more."

Long after Sasuelana had left, Liseth stayed seated in the garden. The picnic basket had been picked up by an acolyte some time ago. Liseth held a beautiful glass globe full of a spicy tea that she sipped as she thought about the future. The rain had diminished, but the clouds remained, holding the world in a wet embrace.

Would the Sea People abuse the powers they were discovering? If there were bad leaders, of course they would. Just imagine what Bayaseth could have done if she'd had the power to drain others. Would she have gone so peacefully if she could have easily attacked instead?

Was that why the Sea People, all the Peoples, had myths instead of history? What terrible wars had their ancestors been involved in? How had they gotten the Sea People to let go of their powers, letting them fall into legend? How did you turn your back on war, and return to peaceful times?

Liseth wasn't certain how it had been accomplished, but she understood that it would be up to her generation to create the new stories for the children and the great-grandchildren to learn from, instead of setting up schools and training them to be as strong themselves.

Chapter Ten

WIND

KA LEM DEMONSTRATED his powers for the elders in a clearing to the west of New Shan Yu. Though many families were rebuilding their homes in the old city, too many had found it heartbreaking to do so. They had quietly relocated south of town instead. Given that the majority of the trade routes reached the new city before making their way to the old one, Ka Lem assumed that the new city would eventually supplant the old one. Possibly just taking on the name as well, and dropping the "New" part of their name.

Overly warm sunlight shone down from a bright blue sky. Thin streams of clouds trailed across the open expanse, as if the day hadn't fully started yet. In his Wind Person form, Ka Lem only smelled the baking grass and sweet smell of the daisies that dotted the plain. He knew that if he transformed, he'd probably still be able to detect the scent of smoke from the burned city in the distance. He heard the distant sound of children playing, as if the world had already righted itself.

Though it was primarily pines that surrounded the open meadow, there were still enough dried leaves in the area that Ka Lem could call upon to form his armor.

The leaves swirled around him with a whispering sound. The scent of decay changed slowly, growing darker and more pungent, like fresh dirt. Brown and yellow leaves changed their color as well, slowly turning blood red. Ka Lem felt energized, as the power of the earth and the wind filled him.

The elders standing to the side sent whispered winds to each other, marveling at the display.

Though it wasn't part of the demonstration, Ka Lem had assured the elders that nothing could penetrate the swirling leaves, not knives, arrows, spears, or even the nets of the Bone People.

He didn't bother demonstrating the killing winds, how he could form himself to become more like a tornado. His winds were too imprecise. He did finish his demonstration with a hint of that, however, swirling the leaves up into a towering funnel before directing them away.

Hi Lop and the rest of the elders seemed impressed. "And you would teach our hunters and warriors how to form such armor?" she asked.

"I would," Ka Lem said. "And then we would go back to the lands of the Bone People and kill all their priests."

He'd explained to the elders exactly what had happened to him, how the priests had been planning on taking the souls of all the Wind People, just as they'd taken the souls of the elk.

"How many of the Wind People will be able to form such an armor?" Hi Lop asked.

Ka Lem shrugged. He honestly didn't know. Nor did he care much. Though the Wind People had already lost so many lives, if they didn't want to lose their souls, they had to go with him, to stop the Bone People once and for all. Every single person who could fight would surely see the urgency.

"Only one in twenty was able to learn Gan Ou's killing winds," Hi Lop said.

Ka Lem turned to Gan Ou, surprised.

"You're not the only one with talents," she told him dryly.

"Of course not, war elder," Ka Lem said deliberately. He was aware that Gan Ou would never be accepted by the regular elders. However, he felt as if the honorific of "war elder" was appropriate, just as she'd been one of the "travel elders" when they'd been facing the great wall.

"After you start training the others, we can discuss returning to the lands of the Bone People," Hi Lop said after a few moments of silent discussion with the rest of the elders, their words carried on winds not directed to Ka Lem's ears.

"We need to return now, this week, if possible," Ka Lem said, stunned. "We have to strike before the Bone People reorganize themselves. Before they kidnap someone else and try again."

Hi Lop gave Ka Lem a look of disapproval.

Instead of bowing his head and acknowledging that he'd spoken out of place, Ka Lem glared back.

Finally, Hi Lop said, "The elders have decided."

"They've made the wrong decision," Ka Lem said bluntly. He knew that wasn't how it was normally done. When someone had an issue with a decision of the elders, they wouldn't just confront the group that way. Instead, they'd work with their parents and just a single elder, to get them to reverse their decision if possible.

These were different times, though.

"We have made our decision," Hi Lop said frostily. The elders all turned and left.

Ka Lem stood there, blinking. Didn't they see their mistake? Didn't they realize that by not returning immediately to the lands of the Bone People, they were potentially dooming the rest of the Wind People?

Before he could race after them, yelling at them, Gan Ou appeared at his side. "Let them be," she said.

"Why?" Ka Lem said, turning his glare to her.

She met his hard look with one of her own. "Who says we have to get their permission?"

Ka Lem stiffened for a moment. Going behind the backs of the elders just wasn't done. He could be ostracized for such an act. Possibly even banished.

Was it worth it to save the Wind People?

Yes.

"What should we do?" Ka Lem asked. Though the one he'd named a war elder was supporting him, it still left a bitter taste in his mouth that the other elders weren't.

"First, you're going to teach some of my cohort that fancy armor of yours," Gan Ou said. "As well as whatever else you have learned."

"I'd like to see what you've accomplished as well," Ka Lem said, his mood softening, the hard knot in his gut loosening.

"Aye, we can do that. But then…" Gan Ou paused and looked out across the plain.

Ka Lem knew that she was looking directly east. Toward the lands of the Bone People.

"And then we do what we have to," Ka Lem finished for her.

"Whatever we have to," she said, agreeing.

KA LEM WAS PLEASED that more of the Wind People seemed to be able to learn the leaf armor than his winds. It meant that his People could be protected, even if they couldn't attack.

Why were there no myths about the leaf armor or the

killing winds? That didn't make sense. Then again, there were very few myths about the Wind People actually using the winds. Most of the myths about the Wind People involved their transforming into animals.

Yet, they were called the Wind People for a reason. They had not been misnamed.

Ka Lem, Gan Ou, and their students—over two hundred of them—practiced openly in a meadow close to New Shan Yu. Ka Lem wasn't about to hide his actions from the elders. He also reasoned that even if he tried to hide, the winds would have told the elders anyway.

The group also prepared for their departure, gathering supplies together. It didn't matter if the elders didn't approve. Ka Lem tried to tell himself that he didn't care. He knew that the Wind People had to strike at the heart of the Bone People sooner rather than later, though. So his group only practiced for a week.

The day before they were to leave was one of the few cloudy days they'd had recently. It was late spring, and most of the days had been dawning sunny and warm. It felt to Ka Lem as though maybe Sune Li approved of their actions, despite the disapproval of the elders.

Ka Lem wasn't surprised to see Hi Lop standing on the edge of the meadow, just under the trees, watching their practice. He didn't hide anything they were doing that day— not the armor, nor the way that they would whip winds around each other, tearing up the ground as they learned focus.

By the time practice finished that last day, most of the grass in the meadow had been ripped up. A haze of dust floated a few feet above the ground, almost as if the clouds had dropped and thickened. Ka Lem didn't bother whisking away the smell of dirt and sweat that rose from him as he walked over to where Hi Lop stood.

"You are determined to walk this path?" Hi Lop asked without preamble. She wore her usual brown robes, her hair curling around her shoulders. It held more gray than Ka Lem remembered. Her walnut-brown face also had more lines creasing the edges than she had before the war, as if she'd aged years over the last few months. She still projected an air of serenity that Ka Lem knew he'd never find.

"We are," Ka Lem said. "We leave in the morning," he added, though he suspected she was well aware of that.

Hi Lop nodded. "The elders have agreed that while we think your actions are excessive, we will not try to stop you, or punish you, for going to attack the priests of the Bone People. There are two conditions, though."

Ka Lem nodded. He was surprised that the elders had even condoned that much. "What are they?" he asked. He found his feet automatically spread out and his knees flexed slightly, as if he was preparing for a blow.

"One, you are not to kill anyone else, unless they attack you. Such as guards," Hi Lop said. "And even then, you should restrain yourselves. Blow them away, or knock them out, but try to leave them alive."

"All right," Ka Lem said. It actually made sense to him that the elders would try to direct his group's attack. "And what else?"

Hi Lop turned away from Ka Lem and looked out over the meadow. "Like you, the elders have been pondering why there aren't any myths about the Wind People using their winds as defense. We think we have an answer."

"I am listening," Ka Lem said formally.

Hi Lop waved her hand, directing Ka Lem's attention toward the meadow. "Normally, I would believe that the land would heal itself in short order. The grass would grow back, as would the flowers. Ants, beetles, other bugs would all come crawling back in a matter of hours. Birds would start pecking shortly, looking for worms."

Ka Lem nodded. All that made sense.

"However, the fields where there were battles—particularly the later ones, where winds were used to drive the Bone People back—have not recovered. Grasses don't grow. Birds avoid the land, flying around the area. Some of the bugs have returned. Not many. Smaller creatures haven't come back either."

"Why is that?" Ka Lem asked, confused.

"I don't know if you'll be able to feel it or not," Hi Lop said. "But the meadow in front of you is mostly dead, now."

"What do you mean?" Ka Lem said. He looked over the open area. Sure, the grass had been ripped up. How had they killed the land itself? It still smelled fresh and fertile, as if the ground just needed the kiss of spring rains to bloom again.

"Ask Gan Ou," Hi Lop said. "She might be the most sensitive of all of you. But this meadow will no longer support the Wind People. It has lost all of its magic."

Ka Lem shook his head. "I don't understand." How could that be?

"The Stone People's land supports the Stone People. There's magic there that they can feel," Hi Lop said. "There's magic here, too, in our land. When you use your winds, you strip the world around you of its power."

Horror washed over Ka Lem. Goosebumps rose all across his shoulders. His stomach knotted, feeling empty.

"Really?" he said, his voice a hoarse whisper. "I…I didn't mean to."

Hi Lop nodded. "We know. We know that you never meant to hurt anyone except our enemies. But once they're defeated, you have to let the winds go. You cannot continue to use them. Not you, nor any in your group."

Ka Lem swallowed against a dry throat. He'd never

thought about letting his winds go. Just the idea of it filled him with dread. He gave a great sigh.

"I will try," he said.

He couldn't promise more than that.

"I will try to follow your strictures. To not kill anyone besides the priests, and to release the winds back into the earth after we're done."

"Thank you," Hi Lop said. "The elders have been divided about your actions. This was the only compromise that we could come up with." She gave him a serene smile. "I believe in you, though. I believe that though you are young, you were raised right. You will do the right thing."

"Thank you," Ka Lem said. "That means a lot to me." At least he now understood the hesitancy of the elders to support his actions.

"May your journey be fruitful and short," Hi Lop said. "May you return wiser and with wonderful stories." She bowed her head to him, then turned and left.

Ka Lem stayed where he was, looking out over the field. He couldn't tell if the ground was dead or not. He believed Hi Lop, though.

What would happen if he couldn't follow their strictures? If he did end up killing someone he shouldn't? Or if he couldn't give up his winds?

Ka Lem felt himself stand up straighter. He could do this. He could do as the elders asked.

He was too stubborn not to.

AS KA LEM was getting ready to sleep that night, a messenger was brought to him. She carried the news from the Stone People, how they'd fought off the Bone People, kicked them out of their lands, and were also about to go to war with them.

Ka Lem hoped that the elders would tell the Stone People to not bother—he and the rest of his warriors could finish off the war and do what needed doing.

Still, it warmed his heart that at least the Stone People recognized what a threat the Bone People were.

No one came to see the fighters off. No priests or priestesses blessed those departing. Everyone's family stayed away, even Ka Lem's. However, around the edges of the meadow they were using as their departure point, they found special packs meant to be carried by the Wind People when they were in their animal form, along with flasks for carrying water.

Hidden, unacknowledged help was better than none at all, though his heart still felt bruised.

It took too much power to travel long distances in wind form. Ka Lem was the strongest of them, and could go the furthest, but even he couldn't travel for an entire day as a wind.

Instead, the group transformed into black-headed geese and took off in ragged Vs, heading straight east. The two hundred plus warriors had divided themselves into a dozen smaller groups, with fifteen or so individuals in each. Gan Ou and some of the others would travel as far east as they could go, then work their way back west again, wreaking havoc as they went, while Ka Lem and his groups would start in the west and work east.

They would blanket the land of the Bone People and kill every priest they came across.

Everyone had agreed to the strictures laid down by the elders. Many had been relieved to be supported by the elders, at least at some level. Ka Lem had no doubt that most would be able to follow those rules, that they'd not only work hard to not kill other Bone People, they'd also gladly let go of their winds when it was all over.

There were only a few who Ka Lem worried about: himself, Gan Ou, her primary student Pan Su, as well as a few others. They appeared the grimmest to him, the most serious. If he were being fanciful, he'd say they almost seemed gray, while everyone else was encased in rainbows of colors.

Then again, he'd always been accused of being a very serious young man, old before his time. Maybe the others had aged as well.

They estimated that it would take two to three months before the two groups would meet in the middle of the land of the Bone People. They would all fly home at that point, and hopefully be able to resume their regular lives.

It took several days for Ka Lem and the others to reach the first town of the Bone People. He hadn't traveled through it when he'd been carted across the lands. Then again, this time, his People had flown fairly far south across the plains before they'd gone east.

The town seemed an odd mix to Ka Lem. While all of the buildings were made of wood, stone, and metal, some of the shutters and doors weren't gray but were painted bright colors. Not all, though. And as far as he could tell, the colors didn't indicate wealth. Still, it seemed an odd mishmash, as though two rival clans lived here, only marginally at peace with one another.

The geese flew over the town scouting first before they attacked. At least the people in the town didn't appear to realize the threat the animals might be.

How long would that last? None of the groups anticipated being able to travel unharassed forever, before the Bone People would realize that they were under attack and started shooting any large animal crossing overhead.

The temple complex was easy to spot. The buildings

had been painted black. It had the most metal fixtures, as well as decorative pieces hanging just under the eaves. It crouched like an ugly tick in the center of the town. A large tower rose out of the center of it, with a balcony around the top, from which the priests could spout their filth.

Ka Lem and his fighters conferred that evening on the best plan of attack, holding off until the dawn. Many of them sent prayers to Sune Li to bless their battle. Ka Lem didn't join them.

Sune Li's light had no place in this dark fight.

They flew into town while fingers of light streaking across the sky, turning the few clouds overhead pink and orange, like any regular day. Ka Lem hadn't bothered eating that morning, his nerves getting the best of him.

The group of geese circled around the temple complex, then descended together, touching down and transforming all at the same time.

Ka Lem tried to pay attention to how the ground felt, to the dirt under the soles of his bare feet. He could instantly tell the difference between being here compared to being in the lands of the Wind People. He hoped the others felt it, felt how parched the land was, how the magic had been drained away by the Bone People.

The smell of dirt and dust rose up with his winds. As well as the sour scent of his fear.

He remembered his helplessness, hanging on the tree as the priests cut him. His skin had mostly healed, but a few of the cuts had scarred. They now glowed white against his dark brown skin.

It was more difficult to attack when nothing was attacking you. It had been three weeks since Ka Lem had fought anything, done anything but sparred and taught others.

Still, Ka Lem remembered. His fury flowed out from him, hopefully infecting those standing beside him.

After a few more moments of working himself up, Ka Lem transformed himself fully into the fighting winds. Those around him called up their own winds as well. They would contain the area. No one would be able to come to the defense of the priests.

Then Ka Lem drove himself forward, tearing the buildings apart, beam by beam.

KA LEM GATHERED with the rest of his warriors on the bank of a small stream just outside of town. The sun baked the ground, turning the air hazy with dust. The water was murky but delightfully cool. Tiny minnows swam in the shallows. It smelled of the bright yellow daisies nearby.

No one in his group had been hurt. The priests hadn't stood a chance. The only ones who might have gotten away were any who hadn't been at the temple. Ka Lem and his group had torn apart the rest, killing them with their winds.

Though Ka Lem didn't have any actual blood on his hands, he still felt it coating his skin. He walked directly into the water, dunking his head and letting the water rinse off the dust. The water soothed his soul though it didn't assuage his guilt.

It was still difficult to kill, even if it was the same damned priests who'd tried to enslave all the Wind People.

The rest of his group splashed into the water with him. Though Ka Lem didn't remember burning anything, it looked to him as though ashes coated the top of the water, floating away from them. He shivered at how cloudy the water now looked, how they were polluting this place as well as killing the land.

Ka Lem was suddenly glad that Hy Yun hadn't been able to come with them, that she hadn't been able to learn either the armor or the killing winds that the rest of the group were able to call.

He knew that the next attack would be easier as the group grew more adept at killing. Some of them were already there, but they'd also been in battles before, many more than he had been. They'd fought the Bone People day after day, seeing their friends die.

Ka Lem understood the elders' proscription against killing anyone other than the priests. It was too easy to grow callous. He couldn't allow that, either in himself or the others.

Ka Lem stepped away from the others and started a loud prayer to Sune Li, praying for the souls of those they'd taken. He splashed in the water, moving in a slow, deliberate dance. The minnows brushed across his legs, as if seeking their own solace.

The rest of the group followed along. It didn't surprise Ka Lem to see that several were crying as they danced, asking for Sune Li to light the way for those who'd gone to meet Ishkra before their time.

Though Ka Lem missed Hy Yun, and would have enjoyed her lively drumming, just the singing and dancing would have to be enough for now.

And eventually, they would all be able to go home.

Or at least that was the plan.

Chapter Eleven

STONE

NOALANON SPENT the next week trying to get a petition signed, to create an official liaison between the Wind and Sea People living in the city and the Stone People. It wouldn't be a full councilmember position—but it would be permanent, and adjunct to the council. They would have to listen to the advice given by the liaison.

No one wanted to focus on that. They were too concerned with the three new councilmembers that would be voted in shortly, as well as the aftermath of the Bone People. Plus the coming war. Noalanon finally had to conclude that while it was a good idea, zir timing wasn't right.

Many, many more people volunteered to go to war than had come forward to travel to the lands of the Wind People, to show their support. The cuts of the Bone People had gone deep. The council had actually started turning away volunteers, though Noalanon knew that wouldn't stop them. Most were equipping themselves and planning on going without being part of the army.

A shortage of containers for minerals struck the marketplace. There was also a shortage of oxen for pulling carts. While some of the Stone People armed themselves with longer spears or bows and arrows, most would travel with whatever knives or weapons they had at hand.

Noalanon felt as though there was a constant rumbling undercurrent at the market, as ze stood with zir petition, unable to get anyone to sign it. The Stone People were angry. Ze had never seen zir people so moved to action before.

It took a lot to start an avalanche of rocks. After it had begun, there wasn't much that was going to stop it until it ran its course.

Noalanon talked with Jolapen about whether or not ze should leave, traveling with the army going to war. Juhala had indicated that a place was available to zir, should ze want it. Jolapen and Noalanon sat in the eating nook that evening, the children long since gone to bed. They both drank warm, sweet tea out of heated stone mugs. The light was low and golden, making the room warm and intimate, with friendly shadows surrounding them.

"I don't want to leave again," Noalanon said, as ze had said before.

"I know," Jolapen said. "But can you stay? Would you regret it?"

Noalanon shook zir head. "I'm not sure," ze said softly. "It shouldn't just be up to me, though."

Jolapen sat for a moment, obviously pondering something.

"Out with it," Noalanon finally told zir.

"The last time you left, you were fooled," Jolapen said slowly "You ended up bringing the king of the Bone People here with you."

Noalanon grimaced. That had been the worst moment of zir entire life.

"Are you afraid that if you go, you'll be fooled again? Tricked somehow?" Jolapen said.

Noalanon couldn't help but gasp. Ze hadn't even considered that. Ze wasn't afraid to leave again. Was ze?

"Or, do you think that by going, you'll somehow make up for that first mistake?" Jolapen said, continuing zir thought. "This war with the Bone People—it isn't because an injustice is being done to a People. Most are going due to a sense of revenge. Nothing more."

Noalanon had to agree with Jolapen's assessment. The Stone People were furious. That constant rumbling undercurrent at the market was anger being expressed. It filled zir with unease.

"I don't think that the Stone People going to war is a bad thing," Jolapen added after a few moments. "I'm not even sure it's the wrong thing to do. But I'd question why *you* were going. You don't have the rage of the others." Ze paused, then reached out and squeezed Noalanon's hand softly before letting it go.

"I know," Noalanon said. "As I said, I don't want to go. But I still might have to."

"Why?" Jolapen said. "Explain it to me so that I can at least understand it, even if the children never will."

Noalanon sighed. "I think you're right, that I want to make up for bringing Forni—the king—here." Ze paused, ordering zir thoughts. "I was here, at the start of this war. With Ka Lem discovering that the elk were no more. I feel as though I need to be there at the end."

"Won't the end actually be here?" Jolapen said. "Once the war is over, our people will need to heal. You can be part of that process now. That's the true end of it all."

Noalanon thought on Jolapen's words long into the night as they lay curled up together, Jolapen holding Noalanon tightly and keeping zir warm.

What zir partner had said was true. The actual end of the war was when zir people started to heal.

Would zir going to war help that healing process? Or just bring more cuts to bear on the Stone People's souls?

THE NEWS of the Wind People's planned attack on the Bone People spread through Killapany quickly the next day. As well as the tales of what the Bone People had originally planned, not just for the Wind People but for all the Peoples, taking their souls and making them slaves. Daleki had died before the Bone People could inflict such pain on them.

The anger in the city reached a fever pitch. Fights broke out that day between people disagreeing about the war. Noalanon had never seen such a thing before. Hadn't ever even heard of it. The Stone People weren't instigators in those sorts of brawl. That was more the purview of the Wind People.

The Stone People had no experience with how to deal with their own rage.

Juhala sent for Noalanon the next morning, asking zir to meet Juhala in zir office. Noalanon went on zir own, turning down Jolapen's offer to escort zir.

If merely walking in zir own city was now dangerous, things really had taken a turn for the worst. The day was clear and cold, and Noalanon felt as if the holy mountain loomed closer than before, as if Kiproary was making zir displeasure known.

Juhala's office was exactly as Noalanon remembered it, cramped yet cozy, filled with books and knickknacks. The window behind his desk still looked out over a beautiful garden, full of graceful statues and picturesque walkways. The only change was that a small painting now hung beside the window. Given the bright red amaryllis done in watercolor, stark yet vivid, Noalanon would guess that the artist had been Sugaoshi. Ze would have to see if ze could also acquire one of the artist's works.

The councilmember wore a light gray shirt that morning, emphasizing zir fine dark skin. It matched zir gray eyes, making them appear wider for once and not always squinting. Ze also wore a serious expression, though Noalanon had to wonder how much of that was an act and how much Juhala actually understood the consequences of what was going on.

"So good to see you," Juhala said, motioning for Noalanon to sit down in the visitor's chair on the other side of zir crowded desk. "I take it you're fully recovered?"

"I am," Noalanon said proudly. Ze hadn't lost time since ze had regained zir wits. Some of the others had taken longer to come back to fully healed, and would sometimes lose themselves and lose time.

"Good," Juhala said. Ze actually looked happy about it. "I'm glad to hear it."

"But you didn't call me here just to talk about my health," Noalanon said.

"True," Juhala said with a sigh.

Noalanon tried to tamp down on zir own impatience. Juhala never wanted to get right to the point. In that, ze was much more of a politician than Noalanon ever would be.

"You've heard the news from the Wind People? How they have a large group of warriors going to fight and kill the priests of the Bone People?"

"I did," Noalanon said. "And I've also heard of fights occurring among our own people."

"Disgraceful," Juhala said. "But…"

"But?" Noalanon prompted when ze didn't continue.

"But understandable," Juhala said. "The Stone People are angry."

Noalanon tried not to roll zir eyes. "I know."

"While the council still supports those going to war, we'd like to direct a few, possibly the majority, to the border instead," Juhala said.

"Why is that?" Noalanon said. "What could they do there?"

"I've been told that you had some success bringing rocks to awareness," Juhala continued.

Noalanon blinked, surprised. Ze hadn't even thought of the little stone container that still sat, empty, on the shelf next to all the others. Ze could suddenly feel it as ze turned zir thoughts toward it. It wasn't a strong feeling, but ze still knew ze could follow the faint thread, even from here. It was like a cool current of rock embedded in the bedrock at zir feet.

"I did have some success," Noalanon said slowly. "Hirshamin had much more, though what ze did was different than what I did."

"Can you explain the differences?" Juhala asked.

"The stone I worked with is more aware," Noalanon said after a bit. "Hirshamin just put zir name on the stones, so that they would act as a beacon, showing the path across the lands to the Bone People."

"Can the stones you waken be used at our borders?" Juhala said. "Would they be able to warn us if the Bone People came back?"

Noalanon shrugged. "I don't know. Maybe."

"You have a place with the army if you'd like," Juhala said. "But I'd like to offer you a different job."

"I'm listening," Noalanon said.

"We're going to try to direct some of the people's anger toward the border," Juhala said. "Get them to pour it into the stones placed there instead. It would go to good use there. Make the border an uneasy place for anyone other than a Stone Person to cross."

Noalanon felt zirself growing still with surprise. It was actually a brilliant idea. It would give the Stone People something to do, something to focus their rage on. Would it be possible for all that emotion to be placed into the stones? Juhala appeared to think so. That would mean draining it from the people, giving them a good avenue for it, making it constructive instead of destructive.

"I would like you to lead one of the teams to the border and back," Juhala said. Ze held up zir hand so that Noalanon would hear the rest of what Juhala had to say. "While you'd still be leaving your home, it wouldn't be for months this time. Just a few weeks at most. And you'd still be in our lands, not crossing into anyone else's territory."

Noalanon nodded. "Let me think on it, talk it over with my partner," ze said, though ze already knew zir answer. Ze would be making one last trip, circumnavigating the territory of the Stone People.

Then ze would return home and never leave again.

THE FIRST GROUPS assigned to protect the borders left before the army did. Noalanon waited on a cart in the marketplace, where so much history had already been made. The area was crowded this time—many had gathered to see them off.

It would take them a little over two weeks to reach the far southern border, or at least as far as they intended to go. There had been some debate concerning what to do about the trade route that went through the southern part of their lands, whether they should declare that the official border or not.

Eventually, the council had agreed with Noalanon that the southern edge of the land was as far as they should go. As for the trade road, which crossed about a day's journey north of the southern border, they might place a few stones on either side of it, so that travelers would merely walk through the lands of the Stone People and wouldn't stray too far from the road.

They didn't bother to bring large rocks with them to the border. The Stone People knew they could find adequate rocks once they reached the area, raising them up from under the ground if necessary. Their carts held minerals, clothing, and camping supplies. However, several of the people in the group did carry smaller stones with them, from their gardens or their homes, planning on setting them at the border as protection.

The more personal the connection, the stronger the awareness could be raised in the rock.

Noalanon had said zir goodbyes to zir family at their home, insisting that they stay there. Now, ze regretted it, seeing how many others were there saying their farewells.

Juhala and Yagakilly did come to say goodbye to zir personally. They both wore formal black vests over their more colorful shirts, the kind that Kinrahsy and Mahletik had normally worn. Maybe it was because they were now the senior-most councilmembers. Or perhaps the vests were just coming into style. The other two former councilmembers were nowhere to be seen. Noalanon had heard a rumor that possibly both of them would be traveling with some of the other border groups, pouring out their own rage into the rocks.

After exchanging pleasantries, Yagakilly pulled out a large black stone from zir pocket and handed it to Noalanon. "For Sugaoshi," ze said gruffly before turning away.

"It came from zir garden," Juhala added quietly before turning away as well.

Noalanon held the warm rock in zir hand. The black

rock felt smooth to the touch, as if it had spent a lot of time tumbled by waves. Faint white streaks ran through it, breaking up the dark color. It felt heavy in zir hands, weighted down with emotion though it wasn't that large. It smelled of salty tears.

Suddenly, Noalanon felt a great outpouring of rage and grief, flowing out of zir and into the stone.

"For Sugaoshi," ze whispered. "And all those who were lost."

<hr>

NOALANON WALKED FORWARD with the other scouts, trying to determine the exact southern border. As there wasn't another People's land that direction, the difference wasn't as clear cut as the border either east or west of the Stone People's lands.

The area they walked across was still quite rocky and mountainous. Grasses grew between the cracks in the rocks, touches of green among the white and gray. Below them lay foothills, a gentle tumbling of rocks off the mountain. Verdant forests lay beyond the hills, the winds carrying the scent of rich earth. A soft creek trickled just to the west, coming out of the higher hills and dropping down into a what appeared to be a peaceful lake, reflecting the blue of the sky and the few white puffy clouds that floated across.

It all looked idyllic, despite the dark anger that the group of Stone People carried with them.

While the scouts tended to hurry, Noalanon took zir time, stepping deliberately, trying to feel the land under zir soles. Ze still walked past the border by three steps and had to turn around to discover where exactly the lands of the Stone People ended and the unclaimed territory began.

The scouts all agreed with zir assessment, though, once ze pointed out the difference.

On *this* side of a line ze couldn't even see in zir mind's eye, there was magic. It supported zir footsteps.

On *that* side, the world was, well, unresponsive would be the best term Noalanon could come up with. It wasn't that it was dead, or actively working against zir. No, it was merely neutral, and didn't have an alignment with anyone.

The rocks looked the same on both sides. As did the dirt and the grass. Almost everyone in the group could feel the difference, though.

Ezekigorn, a miner, traveled with them. Zir child had been killed during the battles. Ze hid zir grief under a jolly exterior. Noalanon and the rest were polite enough to not notice the cracks that appeared.

Once they had determined the line of the border, Ezekigorn began to draw huge boulders out of the ground. It was a type of magic that Noalanon had only ever heard about and had never seen. Ze felt a wonder at the strength of the Stone People, almost enough to ease zir heart.

Ezekigorn would walk along the border, find the next spot, then take a few steps inward, toward the holy mountain. Then ze would close zir eyes and pray for a few moments. Either directly under zir feet, or just in front of zir, a boulder would rise up out of the ground. It would float above the earth for a few moments while the ground underneath solidified, then Ezekigorn would place it back down onto the earth. The sound as the rock lifted was never loud, more of a sifting of sand than a grinding of stones.

Noalanon felt great satisfaction watching Ezekigorn work, as if ze were witnessing the Stone People building their own temple to keep the Bone People out.

Generally the stones Ezekigorn raised were at least three

feet across and two to three feet tall. Occasionally, Ezekigorn would find an exceptionally large rock and draw it up.

Noalanon exclaimed with the others when one such first crested, then continued to rise. It was the size of a small shed. The bottom of it glistened wet in the morning light, while the top half was dry and dusty. It smelled of the river underground that it had been resting in.

That first day, Ezekigorn found three of the huge boulders, each towering over the heads of the Stone People gathered there.

After Ezekigorn raised the rocks, the others in the group did their work. While some prayed, others ground their teeth and growled, each directing their anger into the stone of their choosing.

Noalanon found that ze did have anger to spare, particularly when ze carried Sugaoshi's rock in one hand and reached out to touch one of the border stones with zir other hand. Ze didn't try to raise the awareness of the rock, to mark it as zirs. Instead, ze just put zir rage into the stone, letting it carry that emotion for zir, marking it with zir name so that anyone passing through here would know that this was the territory of the Stone People.

It took the entire group of Stone People working together to mark one of the huge border rocks that Ezekigorn drew up. They stood in a circle around it, each with their palms against the cool stone. Laniaki, a priest who'd traveled with them, led the group in prayers, blessing the stone with the solidity of Kiproary, how ze would stand firm against the threat of the abyss.

When the group was finished that first day, Noalanon looked back with pride over their work. Perhaps ze was just being fanciful, but ze felt as though the border was now distinct, a fine gray line between the featureless hill and the line of stones.

In the morning, all of the Stone People felt tired and drained. Noalanon wasn't sure if the group needed to raise another area of rocks or not, or if they'd already burnt out their anger.

Instead of working more that day, Noalanon had the group pack up camp and move half a day east of their location, closer to the Wind People's territory. Ze worked with the scouts to find the border that afternoon, noting that the southern tip did appear to actually be a tip, as the line of the border was already slanting toward the north slightly, instead of running true east-west.

The next day, Ezekigorn was ready to raise more boulders and the group was looking forward to marking more of their territory. They spent a day doing that, reaching both east and west of the camp. Then they traveled again, continuing east. That became their pattern, working for a day, perhaps a day and a half, then spending a day or two moving camp and getting resettled.

At the first location the group had stopped in, the boulders had been raised somewhat close together, perhaps one every fifty feet or so. As the group grew more efficient, the space between the border stones increased to one every two hundred or more yards.

Noalanon monitored the others closely, particularly in the evenings. They seemed to break themselves into two main campfires at night. One group sang more, had more stories to tell each other, appeared to be healing. The other group was more morose, prayed more, and in general was darker in mood.

When finally only a few remained at the darker camp, Noalanon told everyone they were going back to Killapany. Everyone seemed relieved, even those who hadn't fully healed.

Fog hung low over the hills the next morning. Even the

early birds grew quiet. The air stayed still. Noalanon found zirself taking a hot cup of tea and strolling past camp, looking out over the border.

The sense of the territory of the Stone People came wafting over zir. Even without being able to see very far that morning through the foothills and green grass, ze still knew where the border was. Ze could feel it in zir bones, a comforting feeling, like being wrapped loosely in a warm blanket.

Hadn't that been the point? To direct lines of stones that would warn the others?

Ezekigorn came to stand beside zir, carrying a cup of tea as well. "We've done good work here," ze said quietly.

"I think so, too," Noalanon said. How much did Ezekigorn understand that the rocks guarding the borders were almost secondary to draining out the anger of the Stone People? How was the miner's own grief? Ze appeared to be holding up well—better than ze had been. There weren't as many cracks in zir jolly exterior.

"I may come back out here," Ezekigorn said. "Take another tour of duty."

"Do you need it?" Noalanon asked, prepared to pretend that ze hadn't meant anything by the question.

Ezekigorn gave a hearty belly laugh, that sounded genuine. "Thank you for walking so quietly around me," ze said. "I know it must not have always been easy."

Noalanon merely shrugged. All of the people in the group had had their moments of pain that bit through the normal quiet restraint of their lives. It still welled up, like lava following a fissure to the surface.

"And to answer your question, I honestly don't know," Ezekigorn continued. "I won't, not really, until after I get home and spend a week or so there."

Noalanon nodded. Ze couldn't imagine how hard it must

be to lose a child, particularly to the priests. Ze hadn't learned the full story until recently—how the young person hadn't been killed in the battle, but had died just before, had taken their own life rather than face the constant filth the priests spewed. It wasn't a common event, but it wasn't unique either. More than one of the younger generation had found the bleakness of continuing in the presence of the Bone People too much to bear.

"I hope that you're able to find your hearth quickly and easily," Noalanon said, using the old blessing.

"And you as well," Ezekigorn said. "Go and spend some more time with that partner of yours."

Noalanon smiled. "I am looking forward to that."

"Have you found your peace?" Ezekigorn asked after a few moments of shared solitude, looking out over the foothills as the fog began to melt.

"Like you, I won't know until after I've gone back home," Noalanon said. It was the truth.

How much good had this group done? How much more of these sorts of excursions were necessary to heal the soul of her People?

Those questions, too, needed to be answered before Noalanon could decide.

Chapter Twelve

SEA

LISETH STOOD before the six regents in their land chamber, telling them the news from the Wind People, how they'd already sent an army to attack and kill every priest of the Bone People. The council chamber itself was round, as was the table they all sat at, so that no one sat at the "head" or was considered the most important. Though brilliant lights in glass globes hung from every brown-gold wall, as well as the blue-green ceiling, it still felt dim and closed in.

Maybe that was because the city of Shiboleth was dying. Without a sister water city, the people didn't want to stay. Every week more left, heading for the coastal towns.

The regents looked alternately worried and relieved at the news of the Wind People, how the Bone People were being harried.

"Do you think we could halt the aid that we're giving now?" Regent Ruschyard asked. While Liseth tended to get along best with her, sometimes her practical view of the world got in the way of the bigger picture. Not everything could be measured in money.

"Possibly," Liseth said. She added the news that had

recently arrived from the Stone People, how they weren't taking as large of an army now, and were instead directing their People to strengthen their borders.

"What does that even mean?" Regent Abrassis said.

"They're placing a line of stones around all their territory," Liseth explained. "Stones that are awake. Aware."

"Like in their myths?" Regent Abrassis said.

Liseth nodded. She'd sent a messenger to the part of the Stone People's territory that was closest to the Sea People. A long line of rocks now marked the border. The messenger said that the rocks made her uneasy, as if the stones were watching her.

"So is it time to ask for their help?" Regent Ruschyard said.

Clicking noises came from three of the other regents, as if they were surprised by the question.

"Ask for their help?" Liseth said, unsure of what the regent wanted.

The regents looked at each other, as if trying to decide whether to say anything more or not.

"Oh for the sake of the goddess!" Regent Ruschyard said exasperated. "Would the rest of you wake up and see what's in the waters?"

Liseth waited patiently as the regents held a silent argument in front of her. Fascinating. Three of the regents obviously were in favor of whatever it was that Regent Ruschyard was suggesting. Three were not.

Finally, Regent Solangess nodded, turning her attention toward Liseth. "I know this will not be news to you, but the city of Shiboleth is dying."

Liseth merely nodded. Everyone was already well aware of it. She was surprised, though, that the regents were not merely aware of it, but appeared to have discussed it. Their division made more sense, now. Three of the regents had a plan regarding their population slipping away, and the other three either opposed the plan, or more likely, continued to deny that the city was in trouble at all.

"It's come to our attention that more births are occurring in the smaller villages up and down the coast, in the past few months, than we've had over the course of two years up here in Shiboleth," Regent Solangess continued.

"That's been my reckoning as well," Liseth said. The temple had been keeping a tally. She wasn't sure how the regents knew. What seemed likely was that they'd bribed one of her acolytes for the results instead of doing their own poll.

None of the regents were likely to admit that Bayaseth had been the one to first point that out, while Liseth was willing to give the former priestess at least credit for focusing Liseth's attention.

"We've always taken the warnings of the second age to mean that the Sea People should have both a land and a sea form," the regent continued. "What if it's meant to be a double warning? That the Sea People not only should not just stay in the sea, they also should not gather in large cities?"

Liseth smiled at the regents, thankful once again that she'd kept Sasuelana as a friend and advisor. They'd discussed the possibility earlier, though Liseth hadn't wanted it to be true.

"I believe you may be correct, that there's an alternate interpretation of the official record that we could take," Liseth said. "That the Sea People only flourish when they have more space around them, more room to breathe. Though we find comfort in gathering together, perhaps we need to keep to towns and not cities."

"Which is why I want to ask the Stone People for their help," Regent Ruschyard said. "Help building the new land towns alongside the sea towns."

Now it all made sense to Liseth.

"I believe that the Stone People would welcome the chance to rebuild," Liseth said cautiously. "I think that you should craft a message to their council, see if they're amenable. I do not believe that it's too soon. I think they'd be eager to direct their energies elsewhere."

Regent Ruschyard nodded, obviously taking it on as one of her tasks.

"Is there anything else?" Regent Abrassis said.

Liseth paused, then continued. It was something she thought the regents should know, though Sasuelana had disagreed.

"Of all the acolytes we've tested, only two have been found to have the power to be able to communicate long distances," Liseth said. "I would still like to test more people, to see if they have the ability."

As one, the regents shook their heads.

"Absolutely not," Regent Solangess said.

Liseth bowed her head in acquiescence. She understood the reasons for their refusal to test more people, even though she thought it was a waste. How much more were the Sea People capable of?

But as Sasuelana had pointed out on more than one occasion, just because they could do great deeds didn't mean they should.

Still, Liseth thought it might be handy to train a few, particularly since it appeared that the Sea People were going to be leaving the cities and instead, populating a long line of smaller towns up and down the coast.

LISETH MET with Sasuelana at one of their favorite teashops on the west side of the main market one last time, as

Sasuelana and her family had finally decided to take the plunge and move down the coast.

The market was noticeably quieter, as there were two empty stalls for every occupied one. The merchants appeared disheartened as well. The sounds of the market were muted, with few actively hawking their wares. Even the smell of fresh fish had faded. It filled Liseth with great sadness.

What would happen to the city as her people left? Would some remain? Would it shrink down to just a market town, on the main route to the land of the Stone People? Or would it become a ruin, filled with ghosts, those souls who'd rejected Ishkra's waters?

Sasuelana was actually on time that morning, though she rushed in as she always did, waving at Liseth as she made her way to the counter to order her tea. She was dressed in a better outfit than usual, something newer and not as faded or with as many rips repaired. The soft blue reminded Liseth of a cloudy sky, wisps of white hiding the brilliance behind it.

That might be a good description of Sasuelana, as she was so much more than she seemed.

"Good morning, my dear!" Sasuelana said, sitting down then reaching out to squeeze Liseth's hand. "It's so good to see you. You are looking better."

Liseth looked down at her own outfit—it was her usual off-white gown. "Thank you, I think," she said after a moment.

"You've been looking so tired," Sasuelana said. "I was quite worried. But it appears as though more of the weight has been shifted from your shoulders, finally."

Liseth shrugged. It was true that she'd had twice as much to do, since Bayaseth had been banished. However, as the Sea People had left the underwater city, her workload had finally lightened.

"You look wonderful as well," Liseth said. "How are you?

How are the grandchildren? And the children?" She had learned her lessons of friendship well, though she was dreading trying to find someone else to befriend once Sasuelana left.

Sasuelana gave her a huge smile. "They're all well. Excited about the adventure! Moving to a new place and all. It's a shame we have to leave the city. But no one wants to live here anymore."

Liseth nodded. That had been a large part of the problem —with so many people moving away, no one would buy or rent the old property, therefore families were just abandoning their homes.

It was part of why Shiboleth felt so much like a ghost town, with so many memories just left behind.

"But what are you going to do?" Sasuelana said, peering intently at Liseth. "Are you going to remain here? Or move as well?"

"I don't know," Liseth said. "I don't know if it makes more sense to stay here and fight to keep the temple alive, or to move it somewhere else."

Sasuelana clicked her tongue. "Why move it? Why not recreate it?" she asked.

"Isn't that the same thing?" Liseth said, confused.

"No, my dear," Sasuelana said, reaching out and squeezing Liseth's hand again. "Why should there be such a grand edifice to the goddess when we all carry her in our hearts? Why not, instead of a single temple, there be dozens?"

"That's already occurring," Liseth growled. She didn't bother hiding her disapproval. People were just building temples according to their fancy. Variations on the smile of the goddess were being allowed! Most of the statues still displayed Ishkra as demure, but Liseth had heard of more than one statue showing the goddess actually laughing. Laughing!

"So maybe instead of a single head priestess, there should be dozens as well," Sasuelana said. "You know that part of the problem was that Bayaseth had too much power. Not that you did," Sasuelana hastened to add, "but you've always had a better head on your shoulder than most."

"So I should reform the temple structure?" Liseth said slowly. "Have a council instead of just one or two head priestesses?"

"Exactly!" Sasuelana said. "Maybe a leadership of twelve, that meet three or four times a year, to celebrate the goddess together and to talk of their issues."

"Twice as many priestesses as regents?" Liseth asked. She liked how her sly friend's mind worked.

"Would I suggest something like that?" Sasuelana said, acting much more innocent than her knowing smile. "How are the regents planning on handling the diaspora?"

"They're actually planning on leaving their ancestral homes," Liseth said. "Moving onto large estates down the coast."

Sasuelana clicked in surprise.

"I know!" Liseth said. "It isn't something I would have ever expected either. They haven't gone yet, though. They're waiting until the Stone People come, planning on demanding that their large manors be built first."

Sasuelana snorted her derision. "You're not going to let that happen, are you?" she asked.

"No, we need schools first," Liseth said seriously. "There are so many more children! They will need to be taught."

"Exactly," Sasuelana said. "A whole new generation who won't remember the past."

Liseth sobered instantly. "That's been a concern of mine.

What do we teach them of this war? Of the Bone People? How do we warn them of gathering into large towns?"

"You'll have to rewrite the creation story, of course," Sasuelana said.

"What????" Liseth couldn't help her screech. She couldn't just change that. It wasn't a story. It was their history.

Sasuelana waited patiently until Liseth appeared to have calmed some before she continued. "Myths, stories, are how we teach our people," she said. "You've already allowed that there was an alternate interpretation of the second age, how it wasn't that we just shouldn't live under the sea, but that we should not gather in large cities. Just expand on that in the new teachings."

Liseth shook her head, aghast. How could Sasuelana even suggest such a thing?

And yet…

"Do you believe that there weren't three ages? That the world didn't perish before this? Twice?" Liseth had to ask, trying to determine the depth of her friend's heresy.

"Do I think that there were two ages exactly as described in the myths? Of course not," Sasuelana said coolly. "Do I think that there is Truth, a greater truth, contained in those stories, warnings for the current day? Yes. And those are still true."

Liseth shook her head, feeling as though the solid ground was shifting underneath her like waves. "If I accept your interpretation," she said slowly, "and that changes can be made to our most sacred stories, how would I do it?"

"By breaking up the control of the temple to twelve," she said immediately, "and by giving each priestess more leeway in her individual domain." Sasuelana paused, then added, "Even allowing laughing goddesses, as well as frowning ones. Whatever those people need."

"I don't know," Liseth said. "That's too large of a change."

"It won't happen during the course of one lifetime," Sasuelana said, agreeing. "But you have to set up the initial structure so that those changes can occur. Like water, dripping on stone, transforming a smooth surface into a rutted one."

Liseth nodded. She finally saw the structure that Sasuelana was proposing. It made sense, actually, given that the nature of the Sea People was to swim in smaller schools, as it were.

"Thank you, old friend," Liseth said. "I couldn't have survived this without you."

"Oh, I'm sure you would have," Sasuelana said serenely. "The goddess would have found other ways to take care of you and her people. You will have to trust her, as well as your own heart."

Long after Sasuelana had left, Liseth sat sipping a new cup of warm tea, going over the ideas for the new temple structure in her mind. Yes, she could see how to split up the power among the towns, how to allow for voting, such as the Stone People had for their councilmembers.

It would take years to put into place. And decades before the final pearl was revealed, the base of their power shifted subtly and beautifully, until the Sea People emerged so much stronger than they'd ever been.

It was the work of a lifetime. And Liseth was finally ready for it.

Chapter Thirteen

WIND

KA LEM and his group of warriors made it a point to visit a
body of water after every temple they destroyed. The water
seemed to refresh their souls as well as clean their bodies.
Always, Ka Lem had the impression that he washed ashes
away after every battle, even when there was no fire or
smoke.

They always tried to take the priests by surprise. When
they couldn't, the battles were epic. Ka Lem learned of the
bone armor, as well as the spears the priests could form out
of their wands. Still, the priests fought on a material plane,
while Ka Lem and the others were more elemental.

That afternoon, after the latest battle, when Ka Lem
stepped into the local river, he nearly turned around and
walked right back out of it.

There was something different in this water. It looked
ordinary, a small stream cut into the earth. Sandy banks on
this side, clean and brown. Trees grew down into the mud on
the other side, as if the water had changed course recently,
forced out of its comfortable bank and cutting a new one.
Birds hunting bugs flew down from the trees and skimmed

along the smooth, slow running surface, calling out their warnings. The day itself was warm, no clouds to mar the beautiful sky. Touching the water made the day seem darker suddenly, and colder.

And yet—if Ka Lem had to use one word to describe this water, it was haunted. There were myths of ghosts, those people who refused the healing waters of Ishkra, who instead returned to the earth to cause trouble there.

This stream had that same feeling, as if something lurked under the water that didn't belong there.

Ka Lem turned to look at the others. Like him, they had splashed into the stream then stopped abruptly, not moving. No one had ducked his or her head under the water, or moved to wash away the dust kicked up from the latest battle. They'd been lucky and had taken the priests by surprise, killing most of them without much of a fight.

Water—haunted? Ka Lem asked, using the wind language, directing his words carefully at the others so that no one else would be able to hear.

Most of the group nodded. Ji Zhur, however, shook his head. *Something there*, he said. *Something living.*

Ka Lem nodded, then slowly backed out of the water. The others followed suit.

He had to agree with Ji Zhur's assessment. There was something there, something living in the water that had spooked them all.

But what?

Or who?

WHILE MOST OF the rest of the group made a camp over a mile away, Ka Lem snuck back to watch the stream on his own. He had considered traveling as some sort of dog or wolf, but those weren't common in this area. Instead, he transformed into a large heron who fished at the side of the stream for a while before settling in for the evening.

He didn't have to wait for long. A creature rose out of the water as dusk settled in. It—she?—had the appearance of a Sea Person. She had wide spread eyes, a nose and mouth, as well as arms and legs. She also had a knobby ridge going along the crest of her skull instead of hair.

However, the details were all wrong. Her hands remained elongated, as they'd been in her sea form, with webbing between the fingers. Her feet, too, were more like flippers, long and webbed. She wore a dark matted gown, as if woven out of reeds. She moved fluidly, as if she were more like water solidified rather than hardened bones.

She made her way directly toward the town that Ka Lem and the others had attacked earlier that day. Ka Lem nearly lost sight of her at that point. She cast a shadow over herself, making it difficult to follow her. He transformed himself into a wolf, tracking her by scent alone as she was practically invisible to the eye.

She hesitated at the edge of the town. He would have sworn that like him, she'd been following some sort of track. But it seemed as though the scent had grown diffuse. Eventually she pushed forward, though not as sure as she had been.

She walked directly to the temple. Or where the temple buildings had once stood. The shadow appeared to solidify for a moment, the darkness growing hard as glass.

Was she angry? Fearful? He had no way of knowing.

Then the shadow bled away, following a path to the left, through more than one of the side streets to a poor looking house.

The shadow coalesced there, taking the form of a person again, more or less. She pressed her hands against the wood of the house, the webbed fingers spreading as wide as they could. She grew brighter then, as the wall under her hands grew darker.

Was she sucking light or energy from the building? Or from the people inside?

When she left, Ka Lem marked where the house stood so he could return in the morning, then he followed her. Instead of going back to the stream, she walked out into the plains west of town. The earth here felt dry to Ka Lem, drier than the surrounding area. The night remained quiet, two ghosts passing through, not even stirring the brown grass. Stars shone down from a moonless sky, hard and merciless.

The light from the being intensified as she transformed into a living fountain. That was the only way Ka Lem could think to describe it. She spewed water out from the top of her head and from the tips of her fingers. It even sloughed off her torso.

But it wasn't water. Not really. It glowed too, a faint blue that sank deep into the ground and spread far, as if drawn along an invisible delta.

The earth suddenly felt more alive, less dried out.

Words hissed out across the quiet night as the creature dimmed.

"I sssseee you."

Ka Lem froze. Whatever this creature was, it could communicate. He needed to give it the honor of replying, despite how revolted he was.

"I see you as well," Ka Lem stated as he transformed back into his Wind Person form. He wasn't afraid of this creature, not exactly. He could always race away in the form of a wind if she did attack him.

Or else tear her apart, if she was persistent about it.

"I am…Ajoolesssss," she stated after a moment.

"I am Ka Lem," he said.

"I know," she said. "We met. You ssssaw Lissseth."

"Are you a Sea Person, then?" Ka Lem said after a few moments. He couldn't remember her, though he remembered Liseth, the head priestess of the Sea People.

"Yessss. No. Maybe. More," Ajooless stated. She seemed to have difficulty finding the words, as there were long pauses between each.

"What are you doing?" Ka Lem asked after it appeared that Ajooless had run out of words.

"Killing priests. Like you," she said.

Was that a laugh? It sounded more like an animal chittering. Goosebumps ran across Ka Lem's bare shoulders.

"Yes, like us," Ka Lem admitted slowly. He wasn't ashamed of what they were doing. It was necessary.

It still wasn't easy.

"But you are doing something more," Ka Lem said.

"Kill," Ajooless said, "drain." She gestured to the ground around her. "Then feed."

Understanding dawned slowly on Ka Lem. He knew that his group was draining the world more, due to the wind magic they performed. The Bone People, and in particular, their priests, had stolen much of the power, as well as the life, from the land surrounding them.

Ajooless was somehow draining the magic from the priests and directing it into the land instead.

"How can I help you?" Ka Lem said. While it was important for him and his group to kill the priests, healing the desiccated ground was a higher calling. He assumed that everyone in the group would be able to see that. And most, hopefully, were as tired of the killing as he was.

Ajooless stayed silent for a few moments, swaying with winds that Ka Lem didn't feel. Finally, she spoke, her words clear.

"Kill me," she said, "when the priests are all dead."

Ka Lem felt the world freeze around him. His jaw clenched. Darkness swooped in.

"Why?" he said, his fate clutching his soul as tightly as the bear who lived there.

"I cannot stop," Ajooless admitted. "Once the priests are gone, I will turn against everyone else. Anyone who carries magic."

Her request went directly against the strictures of the elders. He would be killing someone who wasn't a priest. Ajooless probably wouldn't even fight him when he came at her. Possibly the elders would understand—but they probably wouldn't. They'd insist that she could have been saved.

They wouldn't understand the monster that Ajooless had become, that she'd needed to become, in order to end the war, to heal the land, to stop further killings.

"I will do as you ask," Ka Lem said slowly. "I will help you hunt down priests and destroy temples and refill the land with magic."

"Thank you," Ajooless said. "Meet me here at dusk," she added before she appeared to just flow away, a dark mist seeping back into the ground.

Ka Lem let go of a deep breath that he hadn't realized that he'd been holding.

All he'd ever wanted to do was to go back home. Live with his family as a simple teacher. He hadn't wanted to be the one to save the world.

And while he would, indeed, save the world and all its Peoples, he would never be able to return to the place he loved most of all.

THE REST of Ka Lem's group continued east without him,

destroying temples and priests, while Ka Lem and Ajooless wandered far and near, hunting down priests who'd hidden or gotten away from the avenging Wind People. They were easy to spot whenever they congregated together, binding themselves so that they could perform their magic.

Individuals still surely escaped, but Ka Lem was less worried about them. They would learn to never meet together with other priests, or else they'd meet their end.

Ka Lem's flesh grew knife thin, carried on winds and revenge. He knew they hunted for longer than weeks, but shorter than years. Months, perhaps, as the weather grew chilled and the land more barren.

The coming spring would bring so much growth. It would be a bumper crop as the earth expressed its joy in renewed bounty. All the colors of green would spring up in places that had previously been barren and dry. The River People, as Ajooless called him, would finally be able to go home.

As winter drew near, and snow dusted over their footprints, Ka Lem knew that their quest was nearing its end.

Would it happen on the shortest day of the year? When the priests gathered together to celebrate the abyss? To mourn the days growing longer again?

He wasn't sure. Close enough, though, for whatever tales ended up being told about them.

It had been more than a week of fruitless hunting before they decided it was time. They both spent the day praying to their gods and goddesses, thanking them for the life they'd been given.

Ajooless stood in the center of a clear meadow. Small drifts of snow piled up around the edges, though Ka Lem didn't feel the cold. Both moons shone down on them, making the place almost as bright as in daylight. The great bear who lived in Ka Lem's heart stood nearby, watching, her feet shuffling from one side to the other as she danced. Winds not of Ka Lem's making blew around them as Ajooless did her own graceful dance, welcoming the coming of Ishkra's waters.

Ka Lem watched, entranced as well as appalled. Ajooless had grown far beyond a Sea Person, both in her land as well as her water forms. She was both and yet neither at the same time.

When Ajooless nodded for Ka Lem to join her in the meadow, he came with light feet, the bear in him understanding the circle of life and death better than he'd ever grasped it. She was the one who led him close, kept him light on his feet, sharpened his fingernails into long claws that slashed without warning, puncturing an artery in Ajooless' neck, the blood spewing out black and thick, like squid ink across the silvered grass of the plain.

Ka Lem felt himself change as she died, his hands growing into paws, his jaw elongating, muscles building on top of muscles as fat circled his belly and fur covered his bare skin. He growled at the moons as his thoughts drained away and the bear took him deep inside of her own soul, to guard him and protect him, until he remembered, one day, to wake all the way up.

Then the bear left the ravages of the Bone People and headed north, into the snow, where she still might sleep, even to this day.

Chapter Fourteen

STONE

NOALANON SAT in the front cart as they neared Killapany. Ze remembered coming along this path with Forni, knowing that he didn't see the beauty of zir city but figuring that eventually, he would.

No, Forni had never wanted to. He'd come as a conqueror, not as a potential partner. He, and the others, had tried to ruin zir city, cut the heart out of it with their knives, sully their joy with their prayers.

And now—Noalanon wasn't sure what ze was going to see as they neared final turns.

Was this still zir home? Ze had talked with the others on the long cart ride back from the borders to the heart of their territory. Had they done enough? Could they rebuild? Was the foundation still solid?

The road into the city was deliberately kept narrow at a few key chokepoints, to keep the roads safe from attackers. Though no one had honestly thought about attackers coming this far into the lands of the Stone People until they'd already allowed them in.

Sugaoshi had gone to Ishkra's waters with regret tinging

zir soul. The council should never have given the Bone People any access to the city at all.

But no one had imagined just how bad it would get. The Stone People were slow to anger.

Even slower to release their rage.

Was it enough?

Noalanon kept zir eyes straight forward along the road, trying to catch a glimpse of zir city. Ze noticed the guards who blended into the walls, but didn't pay any heed to them.

Ze needed to see zir heart.

Finally, they made their way around the final bend. Without thinking, Noalanon tugged on the reins of the oxen drawing the cart, stopping them in the middle of the road.

Ze could see the spot to the north and east of the center of the city, where a dark shroud still lay. The temple of the Bone People had been built on that spot. When Noalanon had left, the council was still debating what was to be done with the location. A temple of their own, dedicated to Kiproary? A park, full of statues commemorating those who lost their lives during the occupation? Complete obliteration of the location so that no one would ever remember it?

Noalanon suddenly fervently hoped the council would put in a park. Those who had gone to Ishkra before their time should be remembered.

For now, Noalanon's eager eyes sought out the rest of the beauty of zir city. How the straight lines of the roads drew one into the bustling center. The beautiful grays, browns, and blacks of the statuary as well as the buildings. How the shadows played across the neighborhoods, highlighting each in turn.

Yes, this was still zir city.

And hopefully it would be enough, when combined with zir family, to keep zir here.

NOALANON and the others had sent a messenger ahead into Killapany the night before they'd arrived so that those who had families would know that their loved ones had come home.

Ze had *not* expected the main road leading to the marketplace to be lined with people cheering their return, as if they were conquering heroes. Nor had ze anticipated the party-like atmosphere that surrounded the open area, with vendors around the edges selling tea and offering games of chance.

The families of those returning were gathered at the center of the area, along with the councilmembers. Noalanon recognized only Yagakilly and Juhala. The others were new, having been voted in while ze had been gone. Ze found zirself looking forward to meeting them, to learning about them.

Because yes, at some point, ze was going to get into politics zirself.

Then Noalanon felt a tug at zir heart. It wasn't anything as mundane as zir name being called. No, this was a call that ran across the bedrock of zir soul.

That was zir partner over there. Ze looked at Jolapen, smiling. Their three children were waving madly at zir.

Noalanon grinned and waved back, though no one held zir attention like Jolapen. Their bedrock connection was still there, alive and well.

Maybe Noalanon would have to go to the border again, to pour out zir anger.

However, here was zir home. Not just the city. But Jolapen. Zir partner.

Ze was finally home.

Chapter Fifteen

SEA

THE STONE PEOPLE were coming to bury the statue of the goddess. Liseth waited at the door of the main temple for them. No one else was allowed near. The day was filled with mists and rain, as if to hide the deeds they were about to do.

It wasn't respectful to allow Her to fall into ruin, like much of Shiboleth. The sister water city of Sillboden had already been deserted and allowed to fall back into the sea, the magical protective coatings on many of the buildings stripped off as magic and the Sea People left. It would take many years for the stones to tumble down. Liseth suspected that the Sea People would speed the decay, so that what would normally take centuries might only take a decade or so.

The Stone People were going to help Liseth take down the statue of the goddess and bury it in the center of the marketplace, that second home to many of the people of the former city.

The statue was over twenty-five feet tall, with a base of over fifteen feet across. Liseth couldn't face the knowing smile of the goddess, looking down on her, as if Iskra had expected this betrayal all along.

Sasuelana and the others had assured Liseth that it wasn't a betrayal. That leaving the statue and letting it fall into decay was worse.

Liseth still wasn't sure.

She heard the Stone People's cart before she saw them, the clicking of the ox feet along the flat rock pathway. Normally, the splashing fountains would have been louder. But only winds blew through the city now, the souls of those Wind People still searching for priests to take their revenge on.

Or so the rumors went.

Finally, a group of four Stone People on a slow moving cart drew into sight. They were all broad shouldered, with thick limbs, miners sent by the council in Killapany.

They pulled up in front of the ancient round door of the main temple, moving slowly as they got off their cart. They nodded in greeting to Liseth but didn't give her their names. They didn't want to be remembered for doing this deed, though they agreed with the necessity.

Liseth had offered to buy them any equipment that they might need. They had declined, however. They had brought their own ropes and special chisels. As well as their magic.

Solemnly, they entered the temple together. The high ceiling seemed shadowed, veiled with unseen fog. The rows of pews had been removed a long time ago, the wood reclaimed by Wind People, the brass comfort poles scattered to the sister temples that were springing up along the coastal towns.

The Stone People went right to work, not taking time to admire their ancestor's work, how white and smooth the rock had been formed over the solid granite core, how amused the goddess might or might not be by their attention.

They first began by climbing up to the top of the statue, just using hand- and foot-holds that they found magically in the stone. They conferred together, sitting just below Ishkra's graceful neck. Then they began to chisel away at the rock, just where the statue's shoulders started.

Liseth nearly cried out when the head began to topple forward, but stopped herself when the head jerked suddenly, its fall stopped. She hadn't noticed that the Stone People had attached ropes to it, so that it wouldn't fall and smash to the ground. She reminded herself to breathe.

The head was twice the size of the cart that had drawn the four workers here. However, they easily carried the head between them, possibly aided by their magic.

For a moment, Liseth thought the head wouldn't fit through the round opening of the temple door, but somehow the builders squeezed it through. They carried it out of the temple complex, down the main road to the now empty marketplace.

Liseth wondered for a moment if perhaps there should be more people here to watch the passing of the goddess. It was too late for her to change her mind. Just the Stone People, herself, and the floating head of the goddess wound their way through the empty streets.

The Stone People rested the head to one side, the goddess able to watch them open a large hole in the ground, deep and dark, a pit where the goddess would spend the rest of eternity asleep, hopefully dreaming good dreams.

"Is there anything you'd like to say?" one of the Stone People asked Liseth.

She stopped to look at the goddess, the perfect representation of Ishkra's half-land, half-sea form, and knew that no other statue would ever capture the serenity of that smile. Even the laughing statues only got it half right.

"Thank you for all that you've given us," Liseth

whispered, bowing her head. Then she stepped back and indicated for the Stone People to continue.

They floated the head up, then lowered it slowly into the hole they'd already prepared. They didn't cover the goddess's face with dirt so much as absorb the whole head into the ground.

After a soft shifting sound, the head of the goddess had vanished, cocooned in earth.

"Thank you," Liseth said after a moment. She took a deep breath. "Let's get the rest of her."

It took several trips to carry the disassembled parts of the statue to the marketplace to be buried—her arms, the three sections of her torso, each hip separate, as well as the upper and lower parts of her legs.

Liseth left the base of the statue where it had always stood, at the front of the sanctuary. After the Stone People had gone, she spent time alone in the empty building. In her mind's eye, she could see the statue springing back up to life off that base. It was partly why she had left it there.

But she'd also left it there so that people would have a place to come to if they were traveling on pilgrimage. They wouldn't find the statue, but the base would remain.

They could make their own goddess from that, let her become the form that they needed, laughing or sober or something in between.

Finally, Liseth made her way out of the temple, out of Shiboleth, and down to the sea. She'd spend the night in the waters, then swim to the first town, to begin her life as a traveling priestess, one of many.

Eventually, there would be only twelve, or at least, twelve who would be recognized. Like the myths of Sune Li, the Sea People would practice even greater hospitality, because they'd never know who it was who had just shown up at their doorway.

The seeds for change had been planted, as deeply as the goddess's statue that day. Liseth would never be able to go home—home no longer existed for her, or the others.

Though the road would be long, at least she now had hope that for her People's descendants, it would finally be fruitful.

MYTHS OF THE THIRD AGE

The Wind People's Creation Myth

IN THE BEGINNING, Sune Li danced alone in the dark. He/She decided to create companions and gave birth to Gan Zhur and Ban Zhur, the first two people. They asked for solid earth beneath their feet so that they could better dance for the God/Goddess. Sune Li called Kiproary out of the darkness, so that he/she could form the world. Kiproary called Ishkra out of the firmament, so that she could bring the forgetting rains and the waters of rebirth.

Sune Li set his/her lively spark deep in the heart of all living things, so that they might learn their true self and dance always in his/her light.

THE GOD/GODDESS of the Wind People goes by many names. Sune Li, God/Goddess of the flame/light is most common. But frequently the God/Goddess is called

Nameless One, the One God, the Lively One, Bringer of Light and Life.

Sune Li is not represented by any particular form, not embodied in any one creature. The God/Goddess may be represented by a carving of a flame, or a single candle, though in older times, was represented by a circle with radiating lines, representing the sun. But Sune Li is found in all light, not just sunlight.

As a soul ages, one of the goals for a Wind Person is to take every animal shape known, so as to be closer to Sune Li and achieve their own enlightenment, to move beyond physical form so they can just be a spirit, endless as a wind.

The Stone People's Creation Myth

Kiproary drifted in the darkness, a towering mountain in the blackness that existed before the stars. Ze awoke slowly, peering through the abyss and finding none to stare back. Kiproary looked behind Zir and started leaving a trail of bright lights for other to follow, once they took shape themselves. After many adventures, Kiproary decided to settle down. Ze formed the earth around Zir, setting Zir strength down into the core of the world, declaring this place and all the lands as sacred to Zir.

Kiproary created others like Zirself, tall and proud people who took to the firmament to grow. However, they were too static. They didn't move like the animals, but were more like the mountains. Kiproary found that while Ze could move around the stars, Zir people needed help to move on the earth.

So Kiproary invited Sune Li to follow Zir to the earth, to give all creatures movement. The people grew proud. To keep them humble, Kiproary also invited Ishkra and the waters of death and rebirth, as a reminder that the smallest trickle could cut a channel into stone over time, that even the tallest mountain could be reduced into pebbles eventually.

KIPROARY IS MOST OFTEN REPRESENTED by a drawing of a rounded hill. A sharp peak is considered ignorant, or arrogant, or both. Just a pebble placed on a table can sanctify a location. As well as sprinkling dirt finely ground from the holy mountain, where Kiproary first stepped down and walked the firmament.

The Sea People's Creation Myth

Ishkra floated with her siblings through the darkness until they formed the world, each placing their essence into the firmament so that life could begin.

The first people Ishkra birthed had no magic. They were solid as the mountains and as lively as the winds. But they were arrogant. They considered themselves the masters of all, and didn't respect the lives or light of others. They burned the forests, polluted the waters, carved the mountains into little pieces. And they warred with one another constantly, until finally, with the help of the gods, they destroyed themselves utterly. Thus ended the Age of Greed.

The second people Ishkra birthed were strictly a sea people. The waters were wide and plentiful, and the sea people had to live in harmony with their environment, learning quickly that they were dependent on the world and the waters.

But there were too many of them. Ishkra had favored them with multiple births, and they quickly ran out of space. They couldn't survive out of the water, and the gods turned their faces away from those who tried.

Diseases began to run rampant. Even their magic couldn't save them. Eventually, with the help of the gods, the people all died out. Thus ended the Age of the Sea.

The third people Ishkra birthed knew both land and sea. She let first Kiproary, then Sune Li, touch her pregnant belly, so that the Stone and Wind Peoples would be born as well. The Peoples were different, so they would live different lives in separate places. They all had magic, so they would see each other as equals. And they were all lively, so that they could dance and worship the gods.

Ishkra takes all souls and washes them clean at death, giving them another chance to live a pious life. The gods watch and wait, lest the people forget themselves, and decide to challenge the gods. If they do, the world will end in fire and all the Peoples, with the help of the gods, will die. Then the current age, the Third Age, will end.

ISHKRA IS REPRESENTED by a wavy line. Pure water will sanctify a space. Myths revolve around sincerely holy people who can do it through merely spitting. Knowledge and learning are valued above all. The Sea People have many more regular prayers during the day. Leading a pious life is more important to them than any of the other Peoples.

The Bone People's Creation Myth

Valtyr swam through his home, reveling in the absolute darkness. He needed no light, no firm ground, no water to bring him life. The abyss was everything. He needed nothing more.

Still, sometimes Valtyr was lonely. So He allowed others to form in the darkness: Sune Li, Kiproary, and Ishkra. But they didn't celebrate the darkness as He did. They disrespected their home, as well as the being who had allowed them to be born. They celebrated their own individual natures first and foremost, instead of relishing the dark like Valtyr did, or muchless respecting it and giving the abyss its well-deserved prayers.

So Valtyr banished them, sending them out of the darkness and onto the other side, away from the firmament and into the ether.

Occasionally, word of the others traveled across the abyss to Valtyr. It made Him happy to see His children thrive, though none of them acknowledged Him or His place as the greatest of all the gods.

But the Bone People, those who initially stayed behind with Valtyr in the darkness, learned the truth. They knew of the power of the abyss, the true power of death.

Eventually, after many adventures, the Bone People traveled from the abyss into the light, learned to live on the ground instead of swimming between the stars. Valtyr allowed them to be bathed in the waters of forgetfulness between births, though He forbade them to dance as the other Peoples.

The Bone People worshipped Valtyr every waking hour, knowing the absolute power of death over life, relishing the abyss and the dark places.

Valtyr heard the prayers of the other People, of the Wind and Stone and Sea People. Heard their boastfulness, heard their celebrations of light. Finally, He had had enough.

He sent great leaders to the Bone People, powerful leaders who could show them the way, to teach them to use the deaths of others to strengthen themselves.

Now, the Bone People have been called to right the wrongs paid to Valtyr, to show the other Peoples the error of their ways, to bring them all home to the darkness, to swim once again in the waters of the abyss.

Or to bring them death if they refuse.

VALTYR IS REPRESENTED by any sort of bone, though just a line across the dirt will do. All important prayers are done inside, in the dark. Dancing can be punished by death.

The Star-Crossed Lovers

KA LEM WAS BORN a Wind Person, far on the other side of the world. He wanted to be a teacher, however, so he visited all the Peoples, learning their stories and their ways.

The first time Ka Lem saw the sea he felt his heart fill. He hadn't realized that it was empty, before. The waters spoke to him and the very breezes called his name, telling him that he'd arrived home.

Still, Ka Lem stubbornly planned on being a teacher. Until he met Ajooless, one of the temple acolytes.

Though none of the other Wind People, or the Stone People for that matter, would ever think about loving a Sea Person, Ka Lem couldn't help himself. He fell in love with the Sea Person, giving her part of his heart and letting the wild waters claim the rest.

Ajooless wasn't convinced at first. How could a Wind Person love her, a Sea Person? They looked nothing alike. And no one had ever exchanged such a love before.

But Ka Lem stubbornly wooed her, following her into

the sea as a great yellowfin tuna or even an octopus, then returning to the land. He shared his love of the winds with her, transforming into a great eagle and gently carrying her on his back.

Ajooless stubbornly refused to acknowledge her own feelings for Ka Lem, until his learning season was coming to a close. Finally, she confessed her love for him, and they spent a beautiful night holding hands and dancing under the stars.

What were they going to do then? The temples all proclaimed their love an abomination. Their families would not accept them. They had no place to go.

But Ka Lem loved the sea so much, and Ajooless loved the air, and they loved dancing together.

So Ka Lem prayed night and day to Ishkra, begging for her to transform him truly into a Sea Person. He turned his back on his love and went to live on a cave overlooking the ocean for a year and a day, praying the entire time, sustaining himself on the winds alone.

At the end of that time, Ishkra granted his wish. Ka Lem leaped from his cave directly into the sea below him, transforming as he slipped into the water a true Sea Person.

What was Ajooless doing while Ka Lem was praying?

Instead of waiting at the foot of the cliff as he had asked, Ajooless had hiked to the highest mountain at the foot of the Sea People's territory. There, she prayed to Sune Li, begging to be transformed into a Wind Person. She, too, prayed for a year and a day. She lived on the rains and the water carried to her.

At the end of that time, Sune Li granted her wish. Ajooless leaped from her cave into the air, transforming into a Wind Person and a huge black-headed goose and flying away.

She flew directly to the sea, calling out for her love.

Ka Lem heard her call, but he couldn't get out of the water fast enough to reply. He couldn't stick his head up out of the water as a hunter could, he was still too new to being a Sea Person.

Ajooless flew off, thinking that Ka Lem was somewhere else.

Ka Lem, his heart broken, finally reached the surface. He returned to his cave, then dashed himself on the rocks below it. His cry of anguish was picked up by the soulful call of the seagulls, which we still hear even to this day.

Ajooless still flies on the winds along the shore, chasing the gulls and calling for her love, hoping he will return to her some day.

The School

There is a school hidden deep in the woods. There are no roads leading to it. No path through the trees. You can only find it if your need is great enough. Then, the bramble will part and the trail will be clear.

The area around the school is dark, gray, as if the sun can never burn through the fog. The air is always cold and smells of smoke. Ashes regularly float on top of the nearby stream.

Once you have arrived, you'll meet the old teacher, Gan Ou. You will stay at her hearth, eat her stew, and learn about the winds at her feet. Only she can teach you to call the soft breezes of spring that carry the scent of fresh dandelions, or the winter winds that smell of iron and snow.

These sorts of winds are easy to learn and all who find the school can be taught.

Only if you can demonstrate that your need is great will Gan Ou try to teach you the killing winds.

She will tie you to a tree in the big meadow, then start

the dance of one thousand cuts, all the while blasting you with strong winds.

Once your skin is open, and your need is great enough, the winds will soak into your blood and free you from your bonds.

If your need is not enough, by the end of the dance Gan Ou will have to bury yet another body.

The payment for learning the killing winds is thus: after you use them to settle your need, you must return and become the next Gan Ou. Because someone must always be willing to teach the killing winds, once the need is great enough.

Speaking to the Border Stones

Sugaoshi painted day in and day out. Ze used bright colors and the latest techniques. Still, no one would purchase zir paintings. They were too garish, too minimal, and not popular at the time.

Sugaoshi could not put zir anger into zir paintings, though. Zir art was zir joy, how ze showed zir love of Kiproary.

Weeks and months passed. Sugaoshi grew weaker. All zir coins went to zir paints and canvases, not to the minerals ze needed. Ze was too proud to go beg at the temple for something to sustain zir.

Instead, ze spent zir last few coins and bought a cart and oxen. Ze packed up all zir paintings and traveled to the border stones. Once there, ze set up half a dozen paintings, one resting against each stone. Then Sugaoshi prayed to Kiproary, pouring out zir heart and soul, begging for help to make zir paintings better.

Nothing greeted zir cries of pain and anguish. The world grew dark and cold, as if the abyss had followed zir into the bright meadow. Sugaoshi couldn't dance as the Wind People did, nor could ze sing as the Sea People did.

All ze could do was paint.

Sugaoshi started to throw rocks at the canvases surrounding zir, pelting them at first with pebbles but then with larger stones, creating new paintings with the colors of the rocks.

The rocks sank into the paintings, fusing them with the border stones. All of zir anguish was transferred as well. The rocks grew watchful and aware, jealous of their space, not allowing anyone else near.

Still Sugaoshi poured out not only zir grief, but the anguish of all the Stone People. It melted the paintings, pushing the anger and sadness into the very ground itself.

By the time Sugaoshi was finished, ze had nothing left. Ze crumbled into dust that was carried by the winds to the rest of the border stones, waking them to their duty.

Whenever a Stone Person has a time of grief or anger, such as when a loved partner dies, they go tell it to the border stones, for them to carry the emotion, allowing the Stone Person to be lighter on zir feet again. And the border stones keep the Stone People safe from all others, still jealous of their place.

The Twelve-Fold Path

At the end of the third age, twin priestesses ran the two cities of Shiboleth and Sillboden. Both were places of great beauty, but also great sorrow. The Sea People were trapped there. They could sing and dance, and praise the goddess in their own ways, but they couldn't travel to the wild waters, nor could they find the mountains on their own.

The two priestesses reveled in all their power, at being in control of such a large population of the Sea People. They thought that being in the land and sea cities would make them safe, that like a large whale, few creatures could threaten them.

Then the new People came, those who studied the darkness. They formed nets around the cities and none could escape. Then the new People poured their hearts into the abyss, so that it might, in turn, infect the Sea People with darkness, tempting them to turn away from the goddess and the light.

The twin priestesses didn't know what to do. Their great hunters led many battles against the new People, but were always defeated in the end. The Wind and the Stone People tried to help, sending warriors and great magicians, but they, too, could not overcome the darkness.

Eventually, the priestesses realized that while living together as a large group of the Sea People might keep them safe, it was also what hampered them, making them easier to control. Hunters herded schools of fish, not individual guppies.

So the priestesses sent their people off, in ones, or twos, or fours. Such small groups could slip through the nets of the Dark People. They slid away, out of the cities and down the coast, until no one was left except the two priestesses.

One of the twins wanted to stay there forever in her abandoned city, acting as a decoy. Let the Dark People focus their energies on her while the Sea People broke free. The other twin couldn't stand the thought of staying alone in a place and so slipped away in the night, escaping to what she thought was her freedom. Except that none of the others would have her, as she had been responsible for keeping them locked away in the first place. So she died alone in a dark cove, her sorrow forever flavoring the waters near the city of Sillboden, making them unsafe even to this day.

The twin who remained prayed night and day to the

goddess to keep the Sea People safe, to save the souls of those who had left. The goddess entered the twin and led her out of the temple. She grew as large as a statue. Her head brushed the clouds as she walked. Her brilliance shone out over the city, dismantling the nets of the Dark People and banishing their darkness for good.

Then the priestess went to the great grove and laid down, all her energies spent. The earth accepted her, pulling her under the ground for her great sleep.

Some say that if need should arise, she might waken someday, to teach the Sea People the meaning of the light.

The Sea People, now away from the influence of the twin priestesses, vowed to never be kept in a single location again. Instead, they developed the twelve-fold path. A priestess led each of the ways. The Sea People could each be as different as they wanted, seeking the path that they were meant to be on.

And so came the end of the third age, the age of the great cities, with smoke and darkness, as well as the fire of the goddess burning the path clear. The Sea People didn't all die as they had in the earlier ages, but their old lives and their habits did. The Sea People were reborn and never gathered in large cities ever again.

The River People

The River People were born under the earth, in the streams and aquifers buried there. They lived in the darkness, fearing the light. They grew colored like the earth, their skin absorbing the appearance of the soil around them—dark red like wet iron, dark brown like fresh loam, dark gray like buried stone.

They worshipped Kalakami, the great river god, who lived above them and who brought news of the winds and the world in the waters, making the streams aware, dancing in the service of their god.

Though most of the priests for Kalakami were men, there were a few women as well. One was Ajooless, who'd been born with a rare water disease that left her without hair. Her only place was with the temple, as no man would lay with her.

But the god found a special place in his heart for Ajooless, and raised her up above the others, making her his lover for season upon season.

When Kalakami's attentions wandered, as all men's did, Ajooless hatched a plan to get back at the unfaithful god. When she'd been the god's lover, she'd been allowed up on the surface. There was plenty of good earth up there that men might grow tall and strong, as well as many streams and rivers that they could harvest from.

So she tempted the men who lived under the earth to broach the surface, to come out of the darkness and join the light, to breathe the air above instead of the water below.

One by one, individuals listened to Ajooless and left their underground caverns, venturing into the sunlight. They harvested rice from drowned fields, flax and reeds from riverbanks, and fish from every body of water they ran across.

They initially stayed in towns and villages, and there had been talk of gathering together into great cities.

But Kalakami noticed that the River People had moved, and he was angry. He moved as a dark cloud among them, changing their blood so that they could no longer claim the waters as theirs.

The River People banded together to stop their god, to plead for their new lives, to argue that as they grew wealthy, so would their temples.

Kalakami was only partially mollified. He let some of the River People live, but only those who stayed true to the water and didn't gather too often on land. He destroyed their towns and villages, forcing the River People to live either in tents or on boats.

Ajooless was also betrayed in the end, a large bear taking her life and carrying her away to the top of the mountain. From there, her life continues to pour down, feeding the land every spring with life, as long as the River People remember her name and bless her waters.

The Bone People

Valtyr, the great god of the abyss, split himself into two, in order to test the Bone People. While both Valtyrs were still part of the abyss, one half remained true to the light of the stars, holding them up, while the other half turned away and only found the blackest of holes in which to live.

Then both halves went to visit the Bone People. They each wooed the Bone People, trying to see who could gain the most followers, those who followed both the light and the dark, or those who would be drawn to the strictest abyss.

For many years, the two aspects of Valtyr were one, and yet were at war with each other. The Bone People suffered greatly, particularly those who ignored the light. The lands grew dim and the mountains trembled as the Bone People divided. The priests called up dark creatures to do their fighting for them: terrible horses who destroyed the ground with their hooves, the nightmarish elk who breathed fire and shot it from their eyes, and others.

Finally Valtyr of the light realized that the test had gone too far. The Bone People needed a single god to follow.

The dark days that followed destroyed much of not only the population of the Bone People, but their lands as well.

Eventually, the lighter Valtyr won and banished the absolute darkness for good. There needed to be a balance, between the light and the dark, between the abyss and the home.

The Bone People slowly regained their strength, turning away from the absolute darkness, always bracketing the abyss with light.

Finally, after the Bone People secured their hearth did they travel beyond their own lands again, seeking to trade with the other Peoples. They now understood that while their god may have come first, from the abyss, without the other gods there would be no life.

About the Author

Leah Cutter writes page-turning fiction in exotic locations, such as a magical New Orleans, the ancient Orient, Hungary, the Oregon coast, rural Kentucky, Seattle, Minneapolis, and many others.

She writes literary, fantasy, mystery, science fiction, and horror fiction. Her short fiction has been published in magazines like *Alfred Hitchcock's Mystery Magazine* and *Talebones*, anthologies like Fiction River, and on the web. Her long fiction has been published both by New York publishers as well as small presses.

Find Leah's books on Knotted Road Press at (www.KnottedRoadPress.com)

Follow her blog at www.LeahCutter.com.

Reviews

It's true. Reviews help me sell more books. If you've enjoyed this story, please consider leaving a review of it on your favorite site.

Come someplace new…

Are you a traveler? Do you enjoy exploring strange new worlds, new cultures, new people?

Journey into the various lands envisioned by Leah Cutter.

Sign up for my newsletter and I'll start you on your travels with a free copy of my book, *The Island Sampler*.

I will never spam you or use your email for nefarious purposes. You can also unsubscribe at any time.

http://www.LeahCutter.com/newsletter/

About Knotted Road Press

Knotted Road Press fiction specializes in dynamic writing set in mysterious, exotic locations.

Knotted Road Press non-fiction publishes autobiographies, business books, cookbooks, and how-to books with unique voices.

Knotted Road Press creates DRM-free ebooks as well as high-quality print books for readers around the world.

With authors in a variety of genres including literary, poetry, mystery, fantasy, and science fiction, Knotted Road Press has something for everyone.

Knotted Road Press
www.KnottedRoadPress.com